JENIKA SNOW

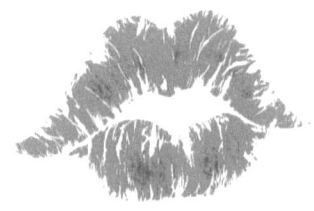

**EVERNIGHT PUBLISHING ®**

<u>www.evernightpublishing.com</u>

Editor: Karyn White

Cover Artist: Sour Cherry Designs

Jacket Design: Jay Aheer

ISBN: 978-1-77339-003-1

JENIKA SNOW

# DEDICATION

To my family for their continued support, to the readers that have stuck through this journey with me from the very beginning, and to the new ones that have joined on the way. Thank you Evernight for giving my stories a home. Without all of you I wouldn't be able to share my characters with you.

JENIKA SNOW

# MALICE'S POSSESSION

## *The Brothers of Menace MC, 1*

**Jenika Snow**

**Copyright © 2014**

## Chapter One

Trevor "Malice" Mason's dick wasn't even hard despite the tits and ass being flaunted around. Although usually his sexual appetite could rival that of a teenager who just found out that sticking his dick in pussy felt good, for a while now he hadn't been feeling the need to let loose. It wasn't because the mother of his son, Molly, was now the old lady of Stinger, a member of the Grizzly MC. He was genuinely happy for them and knew that Stinger treated her and his son well. It would have been a whole other situation if Malice's instincts had told him that the Grizzly wasn't genuine in how he felt toward Molly. Hell, they had even gotten into it because Malice had thought he was still in love with Molly. But that was in the past. Malice hadn't still been in love with her, but just kept to the idea that she was still his. He took a swig of his beer and balanced the bottle on his knee once he was finished.

Someone clapped him on the shoulder, and he looked to the side to see Tuck pulling up a chair and sitting beside him. "You ready for the run tomorrow?"

Malice grunted and nodded. "Yeah. Going to be heading out at nine and ride straight through and we should get into Utah about four in the morning."

"Told Lucien I was able to make it with you the three of you, but he needs me here for that gun trade."

Malice waved off Tuck's response. "It's all good, man. I'd rather have you here to make sure things are good with Dakota." He glanced at Tuck again and saw the older man nod. Tuck wasn't much older than Malice's forty-two years, but the other biker had a lot of life experiences placed on his shoulders, and that showed on his face. The knife scar right over his jugular still showed a bright white even though it had been ten years since he had gotten the damn thing. Tuck had several days' growth on his face, and even though his hair was a light shade there were strands of grey throughout it. Hell, they all had grey, had rough fucking lives, but it was the ones they had chosen, and Malice sure as shit wouldn't trade it for anything in the world.

"Dakota and Molly will be looked after, but you know they got Stinger that watches over them like some kind of protective bastard."

Malice grunted in acknowledgment. "Yeah, but I like my own crew there, too." Tuck nodded and shifted down in his seat. They watched the two women dance and grind on each other, and after a while Tuck spoke again.

"You going mountain man now?" There was a teasing note in Tuck's voice.

Malice chuckled and scratched at his cheeks. He hadn't shaved in at least a week, and the once stubble was now thicker. He certainly wasn't all grizzly bear with a full on beard, but at this rate, especially considering his just not giving a shit attitude, he was headed there in no time at all. "Nah, just not caring about my appearance."

"Well, ain't like you can't get enough pussy around here, even if you look like you been living under a rock."

Malice didn't respond, but even if he'd had something to say one of the club girls came over and straddled Tuck's lap. Her tits were big and fake, and unrestrained by a top. They shook as she moved the top half of her body in front of Tuck's face.

Since several of them were going on a run tomorrow, tonight was about the alcohol, doing some coke and weed, and getting their dicks wet. Malice had never been one to like illicit drugs. Smoking some joints was one thing, but doing lines of blow had never been for him, especially when he had his kid to take care of. He brought his beer bottle to his mouth and took a long swallow. He was currently sporting wood because a fine piece of ass was currently rubbing her tits and G-string covered pussy all over another club woman. They were in the center of the room, their hands all over each other, their tongue down the other's mouths, and their tits pressed so tightly together there had to be indents from their nipples.

"Man, I am going to take that redhead and fuck her so hard she won't be able to walk straight tomorrow."

Malice leaned further back in the leather chair his ass was in and glanced over at The Brothers' VP. Kink looked fucked up already, but kept calling out for the prospect manning the bar to bring over more shots.

"Malice, toss one back with me, brother." Kink grabbed the two shots of whiskey from the prospect and handed one to Malice. "To having a good fucking time, to the health of your kid, and to all we care about." Kink's words were slightly slurred, but then again all of the members of the MC were fucked up beyond recognition.

They clinked their glasses together and tossed the rough liquor back. When more women came forward and started rubbing their shit all over members, jerking the guys off and getting them ready to fuck this was his cue to get the fuck out of here. He clapped Tuck on the shoulder and got out of the couch. Kink was now getting his own private lap dance, but it was more of a "cop a feel" with his fingers up her twat.

Malice was too drunk to drive to his place, so he made his way toward the back of the clubhouse and found a room that wasn't otherwise occupied with people fucking. Shutting the door behind him, he took his cut and shirt off. He sat on the edge of the bed and took his boots off, but didn't bother taking his jeans off. The light was still off, and he lay back on the bed, put his hands behind his head and stared at the ceiling. The shadows from outside moved across it, but for as exhausted and drunk as he was he couldn't fall asleep. The run tomorrow would take him, Kink, and Ruin to Utah to look over some girls that were with another Brothers charter. Normally they didn't swap females around like this, but the Fairview charter was getting heat from the local PD and many of the churches around the small town that were trying to drive them out. A Brothers of Menace club didn't let anyone screw with them, but they also tried to keep the peace, and distancing themselves from the moral police that had swarmed in when the local police had raided their clubhouse and found out they were selling pussy, hadn't gone well for them. So, The River Run charter was taken some of the girls for the time being, and helping out their fellow brothers until shit died down.

Since The Brothers had gotten involved in selling pussy full-time, and staying out of drugs, things were going well. Although they didn't make nearly as much as they had dealing coke, having that kind of heat on the club was bound to get them in trouble. Selling women wasn't legal either, but the authorities were more interested—at this point in time at least—in bigger shit like guns and drugs. They may not deal guns, but that didn't mean they still didn't need weapons to protect the club and the girls that worked for them. It was necessary to have them, and the violence that was associated with their MC, and any of them that they were associated with for that matter, meant they had to do some pretty deplorable shit at times. But Malice couldn't deny that for as bad a rap as The Brothers got in River Run, they did good shit, too. Taking on those beaten and battered prostitutes all those months back and building them a safe haven to recover in was one of the more goodhearted things they had done. They might not do good shit like that all the time, but they weren't always bastards.

The sound of a Harley pulling into the lot had the glare from the lone headlight slashing across the ceiling. He might not have to leave until tomorrow night to pick up the females, but it was already going on three in the morning. Selling flesh was probably pretty fucking low to some people, but what those people didn't understand was that if the women decided to work for them they got protection, safety, and were well cared for. They were not just pussy for sale to the Brothers, but women that had decided on this path for themselves, and had gone into business with the MC. Was prostitution decent work? Maybe money-wise, but it certainly wasn't honorable. He didn't judge what someone else chose to do, though, especially when his own life was filled with plenty of dishonorable things. He closed his eyes, took a deep breath, and let the wave of alcohol that thrummed through his veins take him under so he didn't have to think about any of the shit around him.

He scrubbed his hand over his face and breathed out.

**\*\*\*\***

Adrianna looked over at Phillip as he cut another line of blow on the small mirror in front of him. She was sitting on the floor in the corner, pressed as hard against the wall as she could stand because even thinking of being close to him had bile rising in her throat. Dried blood covered her nose and the side of her mouth from when Phillip had backhanded her because she hadn't brought him his dinner fast enough. She watched as he leaned forward, closed one nostril with his finger, and placed the end of a rolled up dollar bill in the other nostril. He inhaled deeply, and promptly leaned back on the couch and closed his eyes. A few of his junkie friends were already passed out, one on the floor and the other on the chair by the couch. One still had the damn tourniquet wrapped around his bicep from when he had shot up heroin earlier, and the most likely filthy needle hanging from the crook of his arm.

For several months she had subjected herself to this life, but it hadn't always been this nightmare that she feared she'd never wake up from. The first month with Phillip had been great. He had been one of those guys that could captivate a person with a look alone. That was exactly what he had done with her. He had pulled her in, made her trust him, care for him, and then he had slowly started to show himself in small increments. He was a master manipulator, that was so vividly clear, and she hated herself that she had allowed herself to once again be taken advantage of.

The nice dinners and the constant compliments had all just been a disguise to who is truly was. But Adrianna couldn't blame anyone but herself. She had allowed herself to stay in this situation, stupidly thinking that the first time he had put his hands on her was because he had been too drunk to know what he had been doing. And then when he started doing the drugs right in front of her she'd told herself that he had just been stressed out because of losing his job. Threatening to leave had her hoping he might change what he was doing, because she had cared about him, or at least she thought she had. But what she should have done was just leave, not threaten to do it, because all that had gotten her in the end was a lot of pain, some bruises, and broken ribs.

After that things had spiraled downhill faster than she had even been able to comprehend. She could blame a lot of things for why she subjected herself to this: a broken home as a child, and her absentee mother more concerned with the many men she brought home than her or her younger brother. Adrianna could even say that all of that and then losing her brother at the tender age of sixteen to drugs had made her blind to the life she had allowed herself to live. But the truth was she knew what was happening, and even though Phillip had this mean streak when he was high, there were also times he made her feel wanted. At least there *had* been times. Now things were just bad, and she knew that if she didn't leave she would end up another statistic.

"Adrianna, come here." Phillips voice was soft and slurred. He turned his head and looked at her through the slits of his eyes. He was higher than the kite and drunk to boot. "I said come here." He said it a bit more firmly.

She wasn't foolish enough to think just because he seemed lax at the moment because of the drugs that he wouldn't shift into Mr. Hyde. Adrianna picked herself off the floor and moved toward him. She was going to leave, had been planning how to do it without Phillip stopping her, and had been saving what little money she had earned before Phillip had slowly isolated her. It certainly wasn't enough to get her far enough away from him as she would have liked, but she wanted out of this shitty town. She could move to Salt Lake. The bigger city would be a welcome change from the backwards and shitty town she had been living in her whole life. If she didn't get out of her now she wouldn't live to her twenty-third birthday. When she was a few feet from him she stopped.

He stared at her for a few seconds, and then this slow grin spread across his face. Without saying anything he reached down and undid the button of his jeans and slid the zipper down. For how high and drunk he was she was surprised he could even get it up, but he was hard, and his lecherous grin spread even further until he looked like an even grislier version of The Joker. "Suck it."

She glanced at the two pieces of waste of space no more than a few feet from them, and then she looked back at Phillip. Shaking her head and taking a step back, she wasn't going to be subjected to his sick and depraved desires again. His friends roused slightly, but with a few grunts they fell back asleep.

"No, Phillip. I'm done with this." Her face was sore from the slap he had given her, and the bruises on her belly screamed in discomfort when she crossed her arms, shielding herself. "I think it's time for me to leave." She took a step back when his smile faded and he pushed himself up on the couch.

"Time for you to leave?" He said it almost curiously, but she wasn't a fool to think that he wasn't simmering with rage. "You've been with me this long, love all the things I do to you." He smiled again, but this time it was dark and evil.

A shiver worked its way up her spine. She didn't respond, just shook her head again and took another step back.

Phillip stood, put his penis back in his pants, and exhaled. "I was feeling good, Adrianna, really damn good, and I wanted your mouth on me because I thought it would top this wonderful night off." He said it sickly sweet, and rolled his head around on his neck. The sound of his neck cracking, and then of him advancing on her had adrenaline pumping through her veins and the fight or flight instinct kicking in. "You're mine, Adrianna." He stopped and cocked his head to the side. "Unless," he shook his head and chuckled, but it had this dark quality to it. "You're not fucking around on me behind my back, are you?"

She didn't even respond to that ludicrous question. Not only did he make sure she was always within sight of him, if he had to leave her she was to stay with his friends, guarded like she was this piece of property. "I'm no one's, Phillip."

He chuckled again. "But you are." He took another step toward her. "Your body, that laughable amount of money you think you have saved up."

Her heart nearly stopped at his words. "Why, Phillip?"

He looked genuinely curious. "Why what?"

"Why are you doing this, keeping me here like this?" He brought women home all the time, even forced her to watch as he fucked them. Because he seemed to like the junkie girls he brought home more than he did her in the sexual department, she was at least thankful for that. But then there were times like these, where he was wasted out of his mind, and she was the only one around. "You have plenty of others to please you." Her throat was dry, and her heart was beating fast and hard. She was ready to run, and she was ready to fight for her life. For far too long she had subjected herself to this back alley lifestyle, but she wouldn't be defined by it a minute longer.

"But I like having you here, Adrianna. I like knowing that I can do whatever I want with you, whenever I want." He took another step toward her and she took one back. "I like the knowledge that you came from a shitty life, and I was able to mold you to be my perfect fucking cunt. You aren't like the junkie sluts that I stick my dick in. You're my whore, and I intend to keep you that way." He was on her before she could even comprehend what was happening. With his hand around her throat, and his strength climbing as the adrenaline and drugs pumped through his veins fast and hard, Adrianna knew that if she didn't do something drastic this would escalate with her beaten to hell or worse. He lifted her easily off the ground so only the tops of her toes touched the floor.

Opening her mouth, trying to get something out, was an act that she couldn't do. She struggled, clawed at his hand, kicked out and connected with his shin, but still Phillip only seemed to tighten his hold on her harder. Who knew what other drugs he had taken before the alcohol and coke?

"I like knowing that you're mine. All mine. If I want to slap you around, so be it." He took a step forward, and she found herself pressed against the wall. "If I want you to watch while I fuck another whore, I like that option, too." He leaned in and bared his teeth. "You have no one, Adrianna. Before I came along you were barely scraping by. No family, no friends, you're a sad excuse for a human. You're lucky I even want to keep your fat ass around." He let go of her and took a step back. "I mean look at you. You're fat as fuck, and make me sick."

She fell to the floor, gasping for air and blinking back the stars and darkness that had threatened to take her under just seconds before. Lifting her gaze from the ground she looked over at Phillip. He leaned over and stared cutting another line of coke. Adrianna stood, braced her hand on the wall, and then slowly turned her gaze to the razor blade that was sitting on the end table. There was always a razor blade around when junkies lived in the house.

"You'll do best to keep your mouth shut and do what I say." He leaned over, and she heard him inhale the white line. But he wasn't done yet and started cutting another one. "If I want you to wash my fucking laundry and cook my meals, you'll be smart to jump right to it." He leaned over at snorted the next line. She moved over to the end table, her bare feet making no sound on the stained and aged hardwood floor. Reaching out, placing her thumb and forefinger on the edge of the blade, she quietly slid it off the table. Her pulse filled her ears, and she swore she could hear the blood rushing through her veins. Her vision narrowed, and all she could see was Phillip in front of her. What was she actually planning on doing? Killing him? Watching him bleed out? God, this wasn't like her. Before she could place the blade back on the table he turned, and his gaze zeroed in on the razor she held.

"You little fucking cunt." He charged forward and brought his fist across the side of her head.

Stumbling back, Adrianna had to brace her hand on the wall again. Blood filled her mouth, and she started choking on it as it slid down the back of her throat.

"What are you going to do, fucking slice my neck?" He charged forward, but something inside of her snapped. She saw red, tightened her hold on the blade, and waited until he was close enough.

"You piece of shit asshole." The words tumbled out of her mouth at the same time she blindly swung her arm out. Right now she was acting on instinct, not able to focus on anything except surviving. The next sequence of events happened in a blur. She saw the blade go into his flesh and felt his warm blood gush out of him. He swung out at her again, but she ducked and moved. He clutched at his throat, stumbled into the wall, and left a trail of blood in his wake. He started gurgling out his buddies' names, but they didn't move. Adrianna didn't waste any more time, didn't run to the back room to grab her meager belongings. She ran out the front door just as a flash of lightning raced through the sky, and seconds later a crack of thunder echoed around her. She ran fast and hard, and when the rain started down pouring and her feet ached from the pebbles being embedded in them, she kept pushing forward. It felt like her heart would explode from her chest, and all she kept thinking about was if she had killed him. It was the middle of the night, but she'd go to the bank in the morning, withdraw the little bit of money she had, and find out what her next course of action would be. But right now all she wanted to do was put Phillip, and the prison she had allowed herself to be trapped in for too long, as far behind her as her legs could carry her.

## Chapter Two

Malice, Rock, and Ruin all pulled into the rest stop right outside of Fairview town limits. But the sky had opened up, and a horrendous downpour had come down, forcing them to pull off until it ended. Ruin had driven the van and followed behind him and Rock on their bikes. Rock and Ruin were sitting in the truck, and the music they had blasting way too fucking loudly for this hour could be heard even through the closed windows. Malice took out a joint from inside his cut, grabbed a lighter from his back pocket, and lit the end. Inhaling deeply and keeping the smoke in his lungs, he glanced around the deserted strip of road in front of him. He could see the small town of Fairview where The Brothers of Menace Utah charter was located, and saw the few streetlights from the distance. Exhaling the smoke, Malice brought the end of the joint to his mouth again and took another drag. The ride had been long, the road smooth and easy, but he needed this little bit of chemical relaxation.

His bike was parked beside a post that supported the awnings, and he leaned back against it. The wind had the rain moving toward the right, and then a gust pushed it to the left. Right when he was about to take another drag from the joint he saw a flash of white about ten feet away. He stood and took a step away from his bike. Narrowing his eyes and trying to see what in the hell he was looking at, he realized it was a girl walking out in the middle of this shit. He glanced at the van, saw Rock look up at him at the same time, and he pointed over at the girl. Rock elbowed Ruin, and then all three of them were staring at her. She came closer, but it was clear she was out of it. She had to be drunk or high, because who in their right mind walked in this kind of weather in what she was wearing? He stubbed out the joint and watched her more closely. Normally he would have not given two shits about seeing some chick walking in the pouring rain with no shoes on, a tank top, and a pair of cutoff shorts. But for some reason he couldn't stop looking at her, and this strange sensation traveled through him. It was this protective feeling, one that was fierce and strong, and something far different from how he had ever felt, even with Molly. But this was a ludicrous feeling, and one he wasn't about to fucking delve into. He should turn away, walk back over to his bike and get on, storm be fucked, but he didn't move.

She moved closer, as if she was coming right at him. The sound of the van doors opening and closing told him Ruin and Rock had gotten out. The girl didn't look up, but seemed dazed. Her dark hair was plastered to her head, and the long strands stuck to her shoulders. He could see her lips moving now that she was closer, but as if she sensed him watching her, she stopped and looked up at him. For a second all they did was stare at one another, and even from several feet away he could see her eyes were this light blue. He raked his gaze down her body. She shivered, and the rain poured down her body, soaking the white shirt so that it was transparent and her nipples were visible. But what had him curling his fingers into his palms and had rage burning brightly inside of him, was the fact the side of her face had a nasty bruise on the side. Her bottom lip was split, and he had no doubt her face probably had been covered in blood, but the rain had since washed it away.

She looked over at Ruin and Rock who stood right beside him now. "I need help." Her voice was low, but he heard her over the turbulent weather. She took a step forward, stumbled, and he knew she was going down. He moved quickly toward her and caught her before she hit the ground. Water dripped into his face, but he was riveted to the sight of her slate blue colored eyes and couldn't concentrate on anything but her. But he could tell she was passed out. He was up and off the ground with her in his arms and striding toward the van.

"Malice, man, what the fuck are you doing?" Ruin asked.

Malice didn't answer, just carried her to the back. Before he could open the door Rock was there doing it for him. He shifted so he had one knee on the floor of the van, and then he was setting her down on the backseat and pushing the wet strands of her dark hair away from her face.

"Damn, someone beat the shit out of her," Ruin said from behind him, and Malice snapped his head to the side and glared at him over his shoulder.

"Shut the fuck up, Ruin."

The other biker held up his hands. "What in the hell are you going to do with her?"

Malice moved back so he wasn't in the van any longer and stared at her. But after only a second he grabbed a blanket that was in the very back of the vehicle and draped it over her. "We'll take her to the clubhouse."

"I know Marx has a guy that comes in and helps patch up the members. The guy has some kind of medical background."

"Yeah, she definitely needs to be seen, but you think it's good bringing some random woman back to a clubhouse that we aren't even patched in with? I mean they need a heads-up at the very least." Ruin stepped up closer and leaned in so he could get a better look at her. "Especially with all the shit going down with the police and the church people." Ruin turned and looked at Malice. "We know nothing about this chick."

Malice made a low sound in his throat. "I don't fucking care. I'm not about to leave her when she clearly needs to be looked at with all these fucking wounds, and because she asked for help." He shut the door and turned toward them. "I'll call Marx and let him know the change of plans. Maybe he knows who she is and what might have happened." He tilted his chin toward Rock. "Can you call Lucien and let him what the fuck is going on? I don't want him finding out second hand from Marx, or any of the other members of the Fairview charter."

Rock nodded and reached inside of his cut for his cell. The rain had stopped, but Malice wasn't going to wait until it stopped completely before he headed to the clubhouse. He called Marx, let the biker know what was happening and that they were on their way toward them, and hung up. Rock was already off the phone and striding back toward him.

"Lucien's been updated, and he said if we need him or any more members they can head up."

Malice shook his head. "Let's get her situated first, find out what exactly is going on, and if we even want to get involved." Even after Malice said that he knew that there was no way he wasn't going to get involved.

"Come on." Without waiting for them to respond Malice was striding toward his bike and then straddling it. Rock moved beside him and got on his bike, and then Ruin climbed in the van and started it. Malice started his engine, and then Rock was doing the same. They headed out of the rest stop and toward town, and all he could think about was that young girl no more than her early twenties staring up at him with her blue eyes. She had seemed sad and lost, and pleaded with only the softness of her eyes that she needed his help. How in the fuck could Malice turn his back on that? He might be one fucked up asshole on the best of days, and had hurt plenty of bad men in his life, but he wasn't a bastard, especially not to a woman that was hurt and needed him.

They drove though the town, which was still fast asleep, and Malice kept his eyes on the road, but was aware of his surroundings. He didn't see anyone else walking around, and didn't pass any vehicles. Whoever had hurt her wasn't looking for her, at least not right now, or they were doing it on the down low. The passed the small motel that was the center of Fairview and continued to the outskirts of town. Once they took a left and started making their way through the thick forest that surrounded the small Utah community, Malice realized anyone that wanted to give this clubhouse shit would really have to go out of their damn way to do it. But even though he could see the reason why the church going folk might be a little pissed at the fact there was a hardcore MC selling females for a little side action, this was their business. They weren't hurting anyone, the women were consenting, and everyone got paid. It was the way shit worked, and if they couldn't handle it they could shove their issues up their ass.

The Fairview charter's clubhouse gate came into view after about a quarter mile of driving on the long stretch of country road. They pulled to a stop, and once the prospects opened the gate they drove up the driveway that led to the front of the clubhouse. Floodlights were stationed around the perimeter of the property, making every possible point of entry visible. A massive garage had been erected off to the side, and classic rock blasted from the open bay doors. At least twenty guys were outside, either working on bikes, smoking joints, or just bullshitting. But they all seemed to stop what they were doing and watch them approach

Malice pulled his bike to a stop, Rock came up beside up him, and then Ruin cut the van engine. Malice removed his helmet and dismounted, and Rock did the same. Before he could make his way toward the girl in the back of the van he saw Marx striding out of the clubhouse, He had this hard look on his face, and his gaze was trained on the van. Malice strode forward and stopped when he was a couple inches from him.

"Hey, brother." They did the half-hug thing, clapped each other on the back, and then both turned toward the van. Ruin had already opened it, but before the other man could reach in and get her, which was clear he was about to do, Malice was moving forward. "I got her, Ruin." He didn't miss the confused look on the other biker's face, but right now he didn't want to even try to explain what in the hell was going on with him and this woman.

"Come on, let's get her inside," Marx said, and just like that everyone else went back to what they were doing.

Malice followed Marx into the clubhouse, past all the club pussy that was draped over other members, and continued to the back of the building. Marx pushed open one of the doors and gestured for Malice to enter. Once he had her on the bed he forced himself to take a step back. Everyone was silent for a few seconds, and he knew he wasn't the only one that had his gaze locked right on the frail woman on the bed. He ran a hand over his eyes, feeling really damn tired all of a sudden. He shoved his hands in the front pockets of his pants and raked his gaze over her body. She was pretty much covered with the blanket, but her bare feet poked out from the end of the material. The soles were scraped, and there was dried blood now covering them since the rain wasn't washing it away. He looked back at her face, and all that anger rose up once more like a violent wave.

"You know who she is?" Rock was the one to ask Marx

Malice looked over at him and saw the other man shake his head.

"No, but that doesn't mean anything. She could be a wanderer from one of the towns over, or live in the debilitated part of Fairview. Believe it or not, even these country towns have shitty areas."

No, Malice knew about that. Hell, River Run had beautiful parts, but then there were businesses less favorable in the downtown area. "Lucien knows what's going on, but he's holding back until we give him word that we need back-up." It wasn't that the three of them needed the support of their charter, because they were with Marx's crew, and had been close with this charter for a decade. It was more of sticking with the brotherhood and just being there. Also, if things did go bad, meaning Malice found out who had done this to her and dished out the retaliation, his crew would be there for him. They'd be the ones handing him a cloth to wipe off his bloody knuckles.

"What the fuck are we supposed to do with a woman that is beat up to shit?" Marx ground out and moved over to the bed. He stood over her, but didn't say anything for several seconds. "We already got the fuckin' church people down our backs with the pussy for sale, picketing right in front of our clubhouse, and the cops trying to bust us for bullshit reasons. I certainly don't need you bring this shit to our door."

Malice was leaning against the wall with his arms crossed and one foot braced on the wood behind him. "Listen, there wasn't any way I was going to leave her out there. She's obviously running from someone, most likely an ex-boyfriend or husband given what her face looks like. I can be a bastard, but in these kinds of matters I am not going to look the other way."

Marx exhaled loudly and ran his hand over his long, thick white beard. "No, I'm not saying you should have left her, but shit." He then proceeded to run both hands over his long hair. "She's young, really fucking young.

"She could be my kid's age."

They all turned and looked at Beady, who was sitting in one of the chairs with a joint between his lips. "Some motherfucker beat the living hell out of her." Beady looked over at Malice. "She say anything to you before she hit the floor?"

Malice nodded and looked back over at her. "She just asked for my help."

"Well, whatever bastard did this to her needs to get a lesson on how to treat women." Beady stood and walked over to her. The other biker might be one of the meanest assholes around, but he also had a daughter this girl's age, and that had to hit a little too close to home. He reached out and brushed a piece of her still damp hair away from her face. "She's a pretty little thing. Damn shame someone thought it right to do this to her."

Malice didn't miss the way Beady clenched his hand at his side. Hell, it was the same thing Malice was doing—had been doing since he had seen her. He couldn't explain what it was about her that called to the protective male part of him, but seeing her hurt, knowing someone had lifted their hand and beaten her had this homicidal rage filling him. That anger would soon explode and come from him like a murderous demon intent on blood. He couldn't help how he felt, and knew that even trying to figure what the fuck was going on with him was fruitless. He'd get answers from her when she was awake, and then he would have to go out and do some hunting. Vengeance was what he was good at, and the retaliation he was going to deliver to who had harmed her would be sweet and dark pleasure.

## Chapter Three

Adrianna jolted up with a start. Her heart raced, sweat dotted her forehead, and she couldn't catch her breath. The dream that had woken her had been horrible, because it had been too real. In fact, it had felt like she was still living it, like she was back at Phillip's house, fighting for her life, yet knowing she was going to die. But then she had seen that razor blade go into his neck, felt the gush of sickening warm blood cover her, and then fled because she hadn't been able to stand the sight of him dying at her feet. She rubbed her hands over her face, felt the sweat that coated her skin, and breathed out. Dropping her hands to the bed she was on, she looked around. Everything was still so fresh in her mind concerning Phillip, but after that everything was a slight blur. She remember leaving his house, of the rain coming down fast and hard over her, and then of seeing a man standing there watching her. The man's face eluded her, but she remembered his presence, and this sense of danger, but also protection that came from him.

Her face throbbed, her ribs ached, and her feet stung. After pushing away the blanket that covered her, she glanced down at herself. Her clothing was still a little damp, and she was at least thankful that whoever had taken her to this place had at least kept her clothing on. She had a few bruises on her legs, and a look at her feet showed that the bottoms of them were pretty torn up. She grabbed the edge of her shirt and looked at her side, and a nasty bruise covered her ribs. Adrianna knew her face was probably one ugly sight given how painful it felt. Looking around the room didn't help her in gauging where she was, but she didn't feel fear from being at this unusual place. At least that was something to help somewhat ease her already rampant emotions. The room she was in was pretty basic. There was the two person bed she was currently on, a small scarred and old looking desk and chair in the corner, a dresser that also looked like it had seen better days, and a few posters that showed motorcycles and half naked women on them.

She shifted on the bed, and her bare toes touched the cold floor. It would hurt like a bitch to walk, but she couldn't stay in bed when she didn't even know where she was. A glance over her shoulder showed a small window and the darkness that still covered the sky. She needed to get to the bank, withdraw what she had, and then get as far from Fairview as she could. But she hurt pretty badly, and every little move she did had her muscles screaming. There were loud, deep voices right outside of the closed door, but they were too muffled for her to tell what was being said. She braced her hands on the mattress and pushed up so she was standing. The pain was excruciating, but she gritted her teeth and pressed through it. Grabbing the thin blanket that had been covering her, she wrapped it around herself and glanced to her left. There was a partially opened door, and she could see the edge of a toilet right inside. Walking caused even more pain to radiate all the way up her legs, but when she was finally in the bathroom she braced her hands on the counter. With the light now on she stared at herself in the mirror and grimaced. One side of her face was slightly swollen, and a nasty purple bruise was already forming. Her lip was busted, and there was some dried blood on her chin. After turning on the faucet and washing off the copper colored smear, she turned and grabbed the small hand towel that hung on the rack.

When she heard the knock at the bedroom door everything in her stilled. She didn't move for a few seconds, but then leaned to the side slightly so she could see into the bedroom and at the front door. It was pushed open a second later, and she saw a woman come in with a set of clothing, and a bowl on top of that. The woman stopped when she saw the bed empty, and then she glanced around the room.

"Hello?" She moved closer to the bathroom and smiled when she saw Adrianna. The woman had to be in her early thirties, and her clothing suggested she might have been a stripper. "I'm Pam." She held out the stack of clothes and bowl she held. "I was told to bring this to you." When Adrianna didn't answer right away the woman looked at the bed. "I'll just set these things here. I know the doctor was going to come in and check you out once you were awake."

Adrianna swallowed and moved out of the bathroom, but couldn't help but wince with every step she took. The woman didn't cause any red flag to rise inside of Adrianna.

"You need to sit down and have Doc Harley check on your feet." The woman glanced at her face very intently. "And other parts of you." She gestured toward the bed once more. "It's okay. You're safe here."

Before Adrianna could say anything the woman was walking back toward the door. Adrianna wasn't going to sit and wait, and instead followed after her as quickly as she could. The woman had left the door ajar, and when Adrianna pulled it open the rest of the way and leaned out so she could see outside she saw a long hallway that opened up into some kind of great room. She couldn't see anyone, but the voices were even louder now that there weren't any walls closing the noise off. She tightened the blanket around her and moved down the hallway Adrenaline pumped through her veins and dulled some of the pain in her body. Adrianna knew she should be afraid, but she reasoned that surely if they meant to harm her they could have done it already. Besides, she had nowhere else to go, and had no one else to help her. She needed to trust someone, right? She heard the woman start to speak to someone just around the corner, and all other noise seemed to cease. No one spoke once the woman was finished talking, but then there was the sound of several chairs scraping across the floor. Adrianna stopped, her heart now in her throat, and her hands feeling as though she was going to rip through the blanket for how tightly she held it.

As if her body was working without her control, she took a step back, and then another one when she saw three men round the corner. They stopped when they saw her, and although she felt lightheaded, as if she might pass out, Adrianna did not meet the floor. She drew upon her reserve of strength and pressed forward. Instead, she looked into the almost savage face of the biker that was in front of the other two. She could see other men move behind the bikers currently blocking her only way out, but for some reason she didn't feel fear, like she assumed she would have. She was apprehensive, and of course endorphins pumped through her body as she tensed, but that was a natural and automatic reaction. The man in front, only a few feet from her, was possibly the biggest guy she had ever seen. He wore one of those leather vests that she had seen the local biker gang have on when they rode through town. The patch on his left side stated he was the Sergeant at Arms, whatever that meant. She didn't know him, but what she did know was that he was dangerous. That she knew without a doubt.

He took a step closer, and she moved one back. When he held up a hand, almost in a nonthreatening manner, she stopped. "Easy now. You're safe here."

His voice was so deep that a slight shiver worked its way through her body. She glanced over his impossibly wide shoulders and saw there were now five men standing behind him. They all watched her with this hard composure that didn't give anything away, and when she glanced back at the biker right in front of her it was to see he wore the same stoic expression.

"What's your name?" His voice was deep and low. He might be trying to appear nonthreatening, but given his size and the fierce look on his face, it just wasn't working for him.

He had to be at least a foot taller than her five-foot-three frame, and the muscle he was packing under the leather, cotton, and denim had her throat tightening. God, the size of his hands alone had her thinking that he would have no problem crushing whatever was in that massive grasp. His arms, holy hell, his arms were thickly corded with muscles, too. And why was she checking him out like this?

"Your name?" he asked again.

She snapped her gaze up to his face, one that had dark, trimmed scruff covering his jaw, and looked into his eyes. Even from where she stood she could see that his eyes were this odd shade of grey. "Adrianna Carmine." She breathed out and then licked her lips. She saw him run his gaze down the length of her body, stop when he got to her feet, and he stared at them for a suspended second. "Who are you?"

It took him several seconds to answer her, and the longer he stood there staring at her, the more nervous she became. "Malice."

*Malice?* What kind of name was that? He must have seen the confused look on her face because he answered her unspoken question.

"Trevor Mason, but I go by Malice."

Adrianna didn't want to know how he could get a nickname like that, because it seemed violent and dangerous, and implied he probably had done some pretty bad things. She nodded and licked her lips again.

"You're going to cause more harm than what has already been done."

Before she could respond he was right in front of her. She had to crane her neck back just to look in his face, and the scent of leather and something dark and spicy filled her nose. Her heart was beating this fast and hard rhythm at having him so close, but for some reason she couldn't move away. And then he had her in his arms as if she didn't weight anything at all, and was striding back into the room she had just come from. She should have kicked and screamed for him to let her go, but all she could do was stare at his face and keep her mouth shut. She hated that he had this strange control over her, but she also couldn't deny the instant relief she felt now that she was no longer standing.

"Marx, send the doc in." He called over his shoulder without missing a stride. Once back in the room he set her on the edge of the bed and took a step back. He was staring at her face, and she noticed he seemed very tense. Another man came in a minute later carrying a black nylon bag. He didn't look much older than thirty, and although they hadn't said who he was, Adrianna knew he was the doctor. He was too clean cut to be in this biker club; that much was clear by his button down oxford that was this weird shade of green, his cream colored Dockers, and his brown leather penny loafers. He looked like he should be teaching in a university, or giving consultations behind his desk. What he didn't look like he should be doing was hanging out with a bunch of these rough and tough motorcycle men that were twice his size.

"Hi there. I'm Preston." He grabbed a chair that one of the other guys handed him, and set it down in front of her. "Could you help hold up her leg?" He spoke to Malice, and the biker was down on his haunches and holding her leg up a second later.

The feel of his big, calloused hand wrapped loosely around her ankle shouldn't have had her feeling this weird kind of nervousness. Adrianna couldn't help but stare at the long, strong length of his fingers, at how her leg looked so small in his hold, and how she had never thought that part of her body—or any part for that matter—could be considered small. But this man made her feel that way, made this feminine part of her stand up straight and take notice in some kind of primal recognition. This was a man, and she was a woman, and that was what her body and mind were screaming at her.

"These cuts are only superficial, but they will be pretty painful," the doctor looked up at her, "especially if you don't keep your feet up and let them heal." He looked back down at her feet and started cleaning them with various things he grabbed out of his bag.

The room stayed silent, and she glanced up. Not all the men that had been out in the hallway had come into the room, but there were still three standing by the door. They all had on the same identical hard expressions. She slid her gaze to the guy currently holding her ankle and was surprised to see he was staring right at her. His grey eyes watched her intently, as if he could read what was going through her mind. *Good luck with that because I don't even know what is going through my mind.*

"I'd suggest staying off your feet as much as possible for the next day or so." The doctor leaned back in his chair and stared at her. "But I know lying in bed for an extended amount of time will probably start to get a little uncomfortable, too." He had put some bandages on the soles of her feet, and the man holding her legs gently lowered them to the ground. "Although most are superficial, there are a few lacerations that are a bit deeper. You don't need stitches, but adding too much pressure on them will delay the healing process. So, just take it easy." He smiled, and when he lifted his hand she flinched back. It had been an automatic reaction, but it was clear. The doctor stopped, knitted his brows, and then glanced at the guy beside her.

"Sorry," she mumbled out. These men were trying to help her, for whatever reason, and she was letting her emotions take control. Tightening her hands in her lap she straightened and nodded. "Sorry," she said again. "It's just been a bad night."

The doctor nodded and took hold of her chin in between his thumb and forefinger gently. He turned her head to the left, and then to the right. For several seconds he kept her head stationary as he clearly looked at her busted lip and bruise. Maybe she should have felt awkward having these strange men check her out like this, but the truth was she had never had people—much less strangers—help her. Adrianna knew that in time they would want to know what was going on, and of course she would tell them. There was no sense in lying, but maybe they could help her get to someplace else where Phillip could not reach her. Honestly, she didn't know if he was even still alive, and if he was she there was a good chance he'd come after her for payback.

"Not much can be done for the bruising or split lip." Preston let go of her and exhaled loudly. "Just some ice for the minimal swelling." He stared at her for a few seconds, and she felt like he was waiting for her to say something. "Your boyfriend do this to you?" He phrased it like a question, but she could hear in his voice he already knew the answer. She didn't know why she didn't respond right away. "Maybe a husband?"

Adrianna swallowed, and the rawness in her throat from when Phillip had his hands around her seemed to intensify at that moment.

"Can you give us a minute alone?" Malice looked at the doctor. He then looked at her. "You okay with that?"

She looked at him and then at the doctor before finally nodding. "Yeah."

Preston stood and left the room. The other three guys all looked at each other, and then they left, too, as if Malice had given them some kind of silent order. Once the door was shut and it was just the two of them alone in the room, she shifted on the bed and kept her gaze on him. He stood and took a step back, but kept his gaze on her as well.

"Now, how about you tell me what happened so we can see what to do next?" He grabbed the chair that the doctor had been sitting on and sat in it.

"I got hit." The look he gave her was a "No shit" kind of one, and she looked down at her hands. Honestly, she was at a loss as to what to say. Sure, she wanted to go into every sordid little detail that made up her crummy existence, talk about how stupid she was for not seeing the signs right in front of her, but now that she was faced with doing just that a part of her was actually frightened to.

He exhaled roughly and leaned back in the chair. When he crossed his arms she couldn't help but stare at the way his massive arms bulged. "How about we start with the basics?"

She glanced back at his face and nodded. "Okay."

"You're from Fairview?"

She shook her head. "Not originally. I grew up in Littlemore. It's the next town over."

He didn't move, didn't respond, and continued to stare at her as if he wanted her to finish what she had started saying. But then he started speaking instead. "Your boyfriend do that to you." He didn't phrase it as a question, but she found herself nodding as if to answer him.

"Yeah."

He nodded slowly, and she saw the way he gritted his teeth. She saw the way his jaw locked up tight, and she could see the muscle underneath his stubble covered cheek jump. "He do that more than once?" He phrased it like a question again. "You're safe here. No one will hurt you." He leaned forward and braced his forearms on his thighs that were as big and muscular as tree trunks.

She nodded and glanced down at her hands in her lap. She hadn't realized until then that she was twisting her fingers together almost painfully. "No, this isn't the first time, but it is the last." She lifted her head and stared right into his eyes. This man seemed like a cold, hardened person. He didn't show emotion, didn't buffer what he said, and although she knew that he was dangerous just from the air that surrounded him, she did feel safe. It was a very strange feeling to have with this stranger, but it was one she had nonetheless. "That's why I ran, but…" She swallowed again, willing that damn lump in her throat to go down. Without thinking she lifted her hand and loosely circled her neck. It was sore, but certainly not as sore as other parts of her. "I hurt him." Flicking her gaze to his, she saw that he was still sitting as motionless as a statue. Then, very slowly, he leaned back again in his chair. The leather of his biker vest creaked from the movement, and she got a concentrated whiff of whatever cologne he wore, and of the subtle scent of motor oil. It was an odd combination, but strangely enough it was very pleasing.

"You hurt him?" His voice was steady and non-accusing. He held her gaze, never wavering it from her. Although she should have felt like a bug under a microscope from the intensity of it, she felt strangely calm. It was very odd to feel this way given the life she had led, and it was very hard for her to not want to embrace it like a warm blanket.

God, when was the last time she had ever felt like this? Never. She had never felt like this, and that was comforting and frightening. He knew nothing about her aside from the small bits and pieces she had just given him, and adding outside drama to anyone's life wasn't normally what people wanted for themselves. But he wanted to know everything, and she felt obligated to tell him, that it was his right to know since he had saved her. Her heart started beating faster and harder, sweat broke out between her breasts, and she tried to breathe in deeply. As she opened herself up to the memories of what had happened so short a time ago, she started to shake uncontrollably as those emotions started crashing back into her. All she saw was Phillip coming after her, of the blade going through his flesh so easily it was sickening, and the words tumbled from her mouth on their own.

"Hey, it's okay." He reached out as if he meant to touch her, comfort her even, but right before he made contact he curled his fingers into his palm and pulled his hand away. "Take your time."

She nodded, closed her eyes for a second, and told herself that she wasn't back there with Phillip. "I don't know if I killed him." As soon as the words left her she wished she could take them back. Just saying them out loud made the situation even more real. God, what if this guy went to the police? He might have saved her, but who was to say he wouldn't turn her over to the authorities? Just because he looked like some kind of outlaw that broke the law in his leather and wearing a hard expression didn't mean he actually was any of those things. And then she started crying. The tears fell from her even though she tried to stop them. She couldn't remember the last time she cried, couldn't remember the feeling that her world was crashing down around her. With all the shit she had lived through, all the heartache and disappointment she had dealt with, Adrianna had always kept herself in check. But now, all she felt was this unraveling inside of her, and she didn't know why it was claiming her right now.

"Hey."

She wiped a few tears away and looked at him. He looked uncomfortable for a second as he stared at her with knitted brows. A hard, gasping sob left her, and her vision blurred as her tears refused to stop. "I-I'm sorry." Her words were stuttered as they came from her. She felt broken, felt like she didn't have a grasp on reality and was about to float away into nothingness. But maybe that nothingness was what she wanted, because that would be better than being something that didn't mean anything to anyone. Wiping the tears away she sucked in a large lungful of air and turned her head so she was no longer staring him. She had never broken down like this before. She opened her mouth, maybe to tell him just that, but nothing came out. Before she knew what was happening he was sitting on the bed beside her and had his arm around her shoulders. He pulled her in close to him, and she didn't stop herself from resting her head on his shoulder, and clutching at his shirt. Right now she didn't worry about how weird and foolish this was. All Adrianna did was feel the warmth of his big, hard body pressed against hers, and let the sound of his heart beating a steady rhythm calm her.

## Chapter Four

Malice held her, this small woman who was trembling and sobbing against him. He had never been the cuddling, comforting type. Even when he had been with Molly he had never done this shit, but then again Molly had always been a strong, independent woman, and kept a lot of things buried inside of her. This girl was built like a woman, all lush curves that were for a man to hold onto, but right now she seemed so frail and small pressed against him. He shifted on the bed and pulled her even closer to him. She clutched at him, pulled at his cut as she gripped him like her life depended on it. "Hey now." He tried to speak in a soothing voice, but it came out all gruff and shit. He gripped her shoulders and pulled her back so he could look in her face. His heart fucking broke at the sight of the tears that streamed down her cheeks. Something in him shifted, and he found himself brushing away the beads of her sadness with his thumbs. "No one that hurts you is worth your tears." Malice would have probably felt like a fucking pussy on any other occasion for saying these things, but for some reason he didn't feel like that saying them to her.

"I really am sorry about all of this." She sniffled and wiped the rest of her tears away. "I don't just break down like a freak in front of strangers." She smiled, but it was one of those sad smiles that broken his heart even more. "I don't break down at all, so this is totally not me right now." She went to pull away, but Malice wasn't ready to let her go. Not yet at least. When he curled his fingers into her a little more and stopped her retreat she glanced up at him with a bit of confusion, but also relief.

"You're not used to comfort." He didn't state it like a question

She shook her head, but at least she went back to letting him hold her. "No, I'm not."

He wrapped his arms full around her shoulders and just held her. The scent of her surrounded him, and he actually found himself leaning down so that the tip of his nose brushed the top of her head. Malice actually inhaled deeply, smelled her fucking hair like some kind of pervert, but he didn't give a shit. It felt good, and she smelled incredible, like the fresh rain and something sweet and floral. Yeah, sniffing her like some kind of damn animal probably was the creepiest thing he had ever done, but it was what it was, and it felt really damn right. "Truthfully, I'm not used to giving out comfort, so I suppose you and me are one and the same."

She leaned back enough that she could look into his face. "Really?"

He nodded. Malice reached out and pushed her long bangs away from her forehead and tucked them behind her ear. "Yeah, which is probably why I am not in a relationship now." Shit, he hadn't meant to say that out loud, but the words had just come from him on their own. He found it really easy to say things to her, things he normally wouldn't say to anyone, even though he hadn't even spent an hour in her presence. But then again from the moment he held her in that parking lot with the rain pouring down he had felt off balanced with this woman. There was something different about her, and that drew Malice in.

"Looks like we are both pretty screwed up them."

If anyone else would have said that to him he would have taken offense and then beaten their ass, but with Adrianna all he could do was nod and pull her close again. "Yeah, I suppose we are." They stayed in that position for several seconds, but he liked just holding her.

It felt good to have someone close for comfort alone, and not because he needed to get off.

"How does someone get a nickname like Malice anyway?" Her voice was soft, and he could feel her warm, humid breath through the cotton of his shirt.

"I got the name Malice from my brothers."

That was all he was going to say about that, because even though he felt comfortable and different around this woman even after this short time, he also didn't know her.

"You have a lot of siblings?"

At least she didn't probe him. It wasn't like his nickname was some kind of secret, but until he knew more about this woman he did need to remember that she was an outsider.

"I don't mean those kinds of brothers."

"Oh."

She didn't say anything else after that, but he had seen the way she looked at his cut and his Sergeant at Arms patch. Even if someone didn't know much about the MC lifestyle he didn't doubt they would have seen something on TV with all those reality and cable shows on. "Adrianna, how about we get back to what happened?" He felt her tense under his hold, but this needed to be brought to light and the sooner the better.

She did pull away then, and he let her. She shifted so they were now facing each other, and although she didn't speak right away, he didn't press her. Clearly she had gone through a traumatic situation. He didn't know much about her, but seeing her beaten face pissed him the fuck off and made him want to hunt down the motherfucker that had thought it was okay to raise his hand to a woman.

"I've been with Phillip for the past several months. The first month was great. He was charming, was everything that I had never experienced in life, and so I latched on because at the time it felt like the only good thing that had ever happened to me."

Malice knew these types of guys, the bastards that preyed on women because they wanted to control them in the worst of ways. He forced himself to not rush her in telling him where he could find this asshole.

"I never thought of myself as a stupid girl. I mean, I have done things that were questionable. Being with Phillip was the biggest one, but the things he gave me, the affection and comfort when I had never gotten that before, had me wearing these blinders." She sighed and moved back on the bed so she would rest against the wall.

Malice forced himself to keep his gaze on her face, even though he could see out of the corner of his eyes that her shorts were obscenely pushed up her thighs. Was he that much of a sick bastard that he was even remotely thinking of anything sexual given the situation? He scrubbed his hand over his face and exhaled. When he looked back at her it was to see her now watching him intently.

"Long story short, he wasn't who I thought he was. He was this master manipulator. He had me fooled and latched on before I could even realize what was happening." She rested her head on the wall and stared at the ceiling. "He sells and uses drugs. I guess he saw how weak I really was, and knew he could twist me into this pathetic person he wanted." She closed her eyes and gave a humorless laugh.

Malice was barely holding onto his anger. He wanted to find this Phillip bastard and crack his fucking skull open. "The man you are describing is the kind of asshole I have seen countless times over the years. They look for women like you, ones that didn't get to experience the happiness of a good childhood, or ones that were so battered by previous relationships that they took whatever they could get." She could have been the latter, but looking into her eyes Malice didn't think that was the case. She had this strength in her eyes, one that rivaled any man he had ever known, but she didn't recognize her worth. Yeah, she had cried, had gotten the shit kicked out of her, but she was a fighter.

"You know, this is really stereotypical of me, and wrong on every level, but looking at you I would never have guessed you were one of those insightful guys, or one that would help a woman they found." Her cheeks turned pink, and she glanced away as if embarrassed.

"Bikers get a bad rap. A lot of people just think we are these idiots that like kicking ass, working on bikes, drinking beer, and sleeping around. But we aren't just muscle in leather."

She glanced at him again, but didn't say anything.

"Of course we do a lot of stuff that some may deem questionable, but we always have a damn good reason for doing it. And we know our ass from our head." He tried to tease, and although Malice wasn't the joking type, he did want to see her smile. And when she gave him that smile this strange tightening in his gut took residence. "Listen, we don't need to get into all that painful shit." He didn't miss how her shoulders sagged a little. "I just want to know this fucker's full name, and where I can find him."

Adrianna sat up straighter, and he could tell that she had suddenly gotten nervous. She shook her head and glanced at the door, and he thought it was more of an instinctual gesture that she didn't even realize she was doing. "I don't want any trouble. I just want to get what little money I have in the bank when it opens in the morning, and get as far away from Fairview as that money will take me." Her hands started to shake, and she placed them in her lap to try to steady them, but Malice saw the tremor regardless.

He reached out, placed a hand over both of hers that were clasped together, and leaned in so there were only a few inches between them. "Adrianna..." Christ, her name sounded so damn good coming from him, and it felt right saying it, too. "I know it's hard, and I know it is easy for me to say this, but you *are* safe. No one will hurt you again."

"How can you make a guarantee like that?" Her voice was low and breathy, and her fear was laced within the words.

"I can, and I just did. I am not the kind of man that will say something unless I can fucking make sure it is followed through." He stared hard into her eyes, willing her to see that what he said was the truth. "No woman should ever have to feel what you're feeling, and to be honest it makes me want to go out there, find the motherfucker that made you feel this way, and crush his windpipe." He heard her swallow, and although he could have been a bit less crass about the way he said it, this was who he was, and he couldn't change that. "You understand what I am saying, Adrianna?"

She slowly nodded. "Yeah, but I don't want that. I don't want any more violence. I just want to move on, and leave this all behind me."

Christ, he was going to make that punk pay with a lot of blood. "I know, darling, but some things need to be done, yeah?"

She didn't respond for several seconds, but finally she closed her eyes and nodded. "I guess, and even though I don't know if I killed him back there, having more violence thrown around is not what I want. I just want to move on and forget."

"Adrianna, we both know that some things can't be forgotten." Her lashes were so long, and the crescent shape of them looked so dark against her peach colored skin. He lowered his gaze to her lips, saw the plump, red flesh, and this need to kiss her slammed into him. It was wrong, so fucking wrong, but he couldn't push the desire to comfort her in a physical way out of his mind. She slowly opened her eyes again, and the small sound that escaped her told Malice that he wasn't hiding his feelings at all. He saw her eyes widen slightly, and even though she was definitely surprised that he was still so close, and probably by the fierce expression on his face she didn't push him away. He leaned in slightly, but before he could follow through with what he really wanted to fucking do, there was a knock on the door. He pulled back just as the person on the other side opened it.

"Malice?"

He tuned and stared at Rock. The other biker was a smart bastard. He was standing by the doorway, and glanced between them. Yeah, Rock picked up on the vibe that was clearly still bouncing between him and Adrianna, and that was clear by the way he cocked an eyebrow.

"What's up, Rock?" Malice said and then cleared his throat.

"Marx wants to know what the game plan is."

Malice looked at the clock on the bedside table. Shit, they had been in here for almost twenty minutes. He hadn't even realized it had been that long. "I'll be out in a minute."

Rock nodded and didn't loiter around. Once the door was shut once more he turned and looked at her. "Adrianna, who is he, and where can we find him?" Enough of him and his fucked-up arousal taking over

"I don't want any more violence—"

"Men like him need to know that there are consequences to their actions, and it is men like me that will show them what those consequences are." Malice was feeling his anger build once more, and his arousal took a backseat. If the coward bastard Phillip had done something like this to an old lady or someone connected with the MC shit would have gotten ugly already. It wasn't that the MC didn't help people in need, because they did. They might have the reputation as nothing but bastards and trouble, but they didn't just turn their backs on women that were hurt. They might deal with prostitutes, and that was their main source of income, but they also took in hurt women. The safe house they built between Steel Corner and River Run was proof of that.

"But you don't know me, Malice."

Hearing her say his name twisted his gut. "I don't have to know you to see that you're hurt on more than just a physical level." He reached out and cupped the side of her face. Fuck, what the hell was wrong with him? He was acting like some pussy-whipped schoolboy touching her and wanting to avenge her. Shit, they had met only a short while ago, but he always followed his gut on someone, and that was why he wasn't fighting how he felt for Adrianna very hard. It wasn't like him at all to want more from a woman than for her to just warm his bed, and he should back the fuck off, but he couldn't. He wouldn't. After he and Molly split he'd thought she was the only one he could ever have feelings for. He may not be *in* love with her anymore, but he did love her because he was the mother of his son. But staring at Adrianna, seeing her frightened and hurt, but trying to be so strong had his cold heart warming. She was very different from Molly, and not just in the looks department. Where Molly had always been this stubborn thing Adrianna had this vulnerability to her, one that called to the male part of him that wanted to take care of her. She was young, probably almost half his forty years in age, but that didn't matter. All he saw was this woman who needed his help Yeah, he wanted her in a bad fucking way, and one that was wrong, too. She was hurt, scared, and wanted to escape. Wanting and getting were two different things, and he wasn't going to tread that line. Not with her.

She stared at him for several seconds, and although she wasn't saying anything he could see her mind working. "Phillip Montrose." She closed her eyes and breathed in deeply. "He lives over in the bungalow cabins off of Winchester and Broadman." When she opened her eyes there was this stark fear that had nothing to do with what had happened to her. "You're not going to kill him, are you?" She said that last part softly.

He stared at her for a moment, and he was going to say that he planned to do just that, and that he would make sure that Malice's face would be the last one Phillip saw. "Does it matter, Adrianna?" He liked saying her name, liked the way it soothed him in a sense, and the ease at which it rolled off his tongue. This whole situation was not something he was used to. He had helped plenty of women, given the life he led with the MC and the fact their main source of revenue was selling pussy. This, whole situation was not something he was accustomed to. For one thing the first moment he had seen her something in him had halted, and he was forced to take note. And now talking to her, hearing her story, and wanting to hold her close and make sure no one every messed with her again after just meeting her… He shook his head. This was fucked up in every possible way.

"Yeah, it does matter."

Malice shifted back on the bed so he was facing the door now. His instincts told him to just go and fuck

49

this guy up without even caring if he died in the end. A brutal and ruthless attitude to have, but that was the kind of man he was, and the kind of man he had to be in his position within the MC. Malice didn't do anything half-assed, and especially not when he felt this passionate about something. "Why wouldn't you want a man that beat you up to have his life ended?" He turned just his head and looked at her.

She stayed silent for a few seconds, stared at her fingers, and then finally looked back at him. "I might have already ended his life, and although he deserved it, the very idea that I could have killed someone makes me sick. If he is alive, I don't want his blood on anyone's hands, least of all yours."

"If he did this to you, chances are he has done it before, and will continue to do it." He knew his voice was hard and unyielding, and he didn't mean to make her uncomfortable, but he had no softness when it came to shit like this.

"You're right." She licked her lips, glanced at the clock, and then looked back at him. "It's late. Would it be okay if I stayed here until the morning?" He didn't miss the fact she averted the conversation to something far more neutral. She looked at her feet that had bandages around the soles. "I just need to rest for a little bit. My feet and face are killing me."

And just like that his anger faded to the back as his concern rose up. "I wouldn't have had you stay anywhere else. The club is the safest place you could be right now. Lay back. I'll get you something for the pain." He stood and took a few steps toward the door, but stopped and glanced over his shoulder. She was on her back now and reaching for the blanket. "And Adrianna?"

She paused and looked at him.

"You're no trouble. If it wasn't okay for you to be here you wouldn't."

She slowly nodded. "Thank you, and please tell everyone else I said that."

He gave a brisk nod, faced forward once more, and went to get her something to help her discomfort.

## Chapter Five

The following day Adrianna sat at the scarred wooden table in the great room of what she had found out was The Brothers of Menace clubhouse in Fairview. She didn't know much about the motorcycle lifestyle, but after listening to the bikers in this club talk, she had learned quite a bit in a very short amount of time. Some might have said she was living under a rock by not realizing where she had been right off the bat, but to be honest her life hadn't given her much freedom to think about other things that didn't involve staying alive, figuratively and literally speaking. Malice sat beside her, but he had his chair positioned so it was at an odd angle, with his body facing her. He rested an elbow on the stained and chipped wood, and stared at her. His position was a bit intimidating.

"You're feeling better?"

She looked back at Marx, the president of this MC, and nodded in response to his question. "Yes, thank you. The pills Malice gave me last night helped me sleep." She shifted on the chair and took note that the five guys that were currently seated at the table with her were big, scary looking, and had their attention solely on her. The doctor had also given her some medicine, and whatever they were had helped her feet feel a lot better. Of course there was still discomfort when she walked, but it wasn't nearly as bad as it had been yesterday. Or maybe she had just needed a really good night's sleep? She had certainly gotten that last night, too. "I should have thought before just running out of there, but I just reacted."

What had happened wasn't a secret. She had told Malice, and then when she had woken up over an hour ago and sat down in front of all of them she had repeated the same thing. She also hadn't missed the way they looked at each other after she had told them everything Phillip had done to her. Well, most of what he had done. She hadn't gone into detail about her relationship with him over the last several months. Some things were just better left in the past, and, besides, she'd only had one good month with him. Truthfully she was ashamed that she had been such an idiot to fall for his manipulation in the first place.

"I'm glad you're feeling better, but that prick and what he did need to be put in the past. Let's focus on the future." Marx leaned back in the chair, and it creaked slightly from his weight.

All of these men were huge, scary, and didn't take shit from anyone, that much was clear. It wasn't just the bulk of denim and leather that they wore, but the strength and power that came from them.

"So, what are your plans after you get your money out of the bank?"

She looked at the clock. The bank wouldn't open for another hour, and although she only had a few hundred dollars in there, she was glad she had at least been smart enough to start an account years ago. There wasn't much money in it, because anything she had earned had gone to support her, and her brother when he had been alive. "I don't know honestly. All I know is I want to get as far away from Fairview as I can with what little money I have."

Marx glanced at Malice, and she watched some kind of silent communication going on between them. She had heard a small bit of conversation where she pieced together that Malice and a few other men had come up here from Colorado to take care of some kind of business. What that business was clearly wasn't known to her, and Adrianna didn't know if she even wanted to know. There was a banging noise that came from the other side of the clubhouse house in one of the backrooms. She glanced down the hallway at where the sound came from, but Marx speaking again drew her attention.

"And how much are we talking about that you have to work with?" Marx asked.

"Not a lot, less than five hundred dollars, but that's enough to get me a good distance away." At least she hoped. She had no clue what the cost of a bus ticket would be, but surely it wouldn't be that expensive, especially given the fact it was one-way.

Marx started tapping his fingers on the table. "You have any skills?"

"Skills?"

"No." Everyone turned and stared at Malice. He had said that one word so forcefully that her heart started beating faster because of it.

"No what?" Marx leaned forward and braced his arms on the table as he addressed Malice.

"You know exactly what I am refusing, Marx." The two men stared at each other for several seconds after Malice spoke.

"The way I see it we put her up for a whole night, gave her some of our narcotics, and had to make a call into the doc to come and check her out. I think we are owed."

Adrianna felt this frigid blast slam into her, and she realized it came from Malice. She had no clue what was happening, but she didn't want these guys fighting over her. "I can pay you for letting me stay here." Even though she had little to her name, they *had* helped her, and she knew better than anyone that things in this world didn't come for free.

"Honey, this club makes money a different kind of way," Marx said and grinned at her.

"I said no," Malice said again, but this time it was harder, and fiercer.

Marx held up his hands in surrender. "All right, all right. No need to get possessive, Malice. I was just putting that option on the table." He looked over at her, braced his hands on the table, and then pushed himself up so he was standing. "I was only teasing you about paying, honey." He looked over at Malice. "Everything's all good, brother." There was a tense moment that passed, and then Malice nodded and seemed to relax marginally. "You're taking the shipment with you at nightfall?"

Malice nodded, and Marx grunted in response.

"We'll keep shit on the quiet while everything is getting set up. No need to alert the cult fanatics to what's going on. They'll have their signs and be shouting that we are cruel and immoral motherfuckers." He glanced at Adrianna, winked, and turned to leave. The other man that had been sitting beside him got up and left, too.

They left out of the front, and then it was just her, Malice, and the two bikers that she knew were with him. The silence stretched on, and finally she spoke. "I'm sorry if I caused any problems." Marx might have acted like he was teasing, but Adrianna knew that Malice hadn't liked whatever he had been getting at.

Malice said something low to the men sitting beside him, and a second later they rose and disappeared down the back hall where she had heard the noise come from. Keeping her gaze locked on them, she watched as they pushed a door open, and she swore she heard women talking. She felt the hair on the back of her neck standing on end, and she turned to see Malice staring at her. She didn't know why she had felt that way just then, because it wasn't like there weren't women walking around in barely there clothing and cleaning up, but something about the women she had heard in the back made her a bit unsettled.

"You're not any trouble," he said, breaking up the weird vibe that was filling the room.

"Are you sure? Because I know I kind of created this whole big shit-storm by intruding in on your lives."

The corner of his mouth kicked up, and she felt this warmth fill her. It started at her toes and worked its way up her whole body. He shrugged and braced an arm over the back of his chair. "Believe me, this is one of the smallest inconveniences we have ever had."

Adrianna swallowed and nodded, but she couldn't get Marx's words out of her head. "Can I ask what exactly he was saying about payment?" There was a part of her that didn't want to know, but then again there was another part that already had an idea of what Marx had been referring to. The sound of glasses clanking had her looking to her right and seeing a woman drying dishes behind the bar. Another one, a bit younger than the barmaid, came out of a back room with a crate of beer. She wore a cutoff tank, had teased bleached hair with dark roots, and looked the worse for wear. When she looked back at Malice it was to see him wearing that same hard expression. He looked pissed, but before she could say anything he started speaking.

"I'm sure if you think about it hard enough you can come up with what Marx was implying." He ground his teeth, and she saw that his hands were in tight balls on top of the table.

"Sex." She didn't phrase it like a question, and Malice didn't respond, but he did clench his jaw even harder. This reaction from him was odd, but maybe there was more of a history between the two men?

"Sex, and more."

"More?" She sat up straighter, and her mind worked on all that "more" could mean.

"More, Adrianna. As in spreading your legs for a john and making the club money." He stood suddenly and started pacing. "Willingly of course, because the club doesn't force women to have sex with men. We can be bastards, but we aren't sck fucking men that like to see women hurt." He seemed so off kilter, and she may not know him very well, but for some reason Adrianna had a feeling this wasn't how he normally was.

Her pulse pounded faster, but she wasn't surprised by this revelation. In fact, this wasn't even a new topic for her. She had seen her mother whore herself plenty of times to the men that came and went through their shack of a house. It had been a part of her life, and how sad was that? "Malice?"

He stopped packing and stared at her, and for a second that was all they did. "Yeah, Adrianna?"

The way he said her name shouldn't have had this tingle moving around in her belly. She opened her mouth, not exactly sure what she was going to say, but the sound of glass breaking on the ground saved her from saying something monumentally stupid.

"Sorry, guys."

Adrianna looked over at the young woman that had dropped the glass. She smiled and waved at Adrianna, and she found herself smiling back. She felt so weird when a stranger showed her any kind of kindness.

"If you're ready I can take you to the bank," Malice said, and she looked back at him. Leaving right now sounded like the best thing to do, especially considering the offer of having sex with random men. She stood, smiled to soften the situation, and waited for him to say something else. Maybe he was going through personal problems, and having her to deal with, and this need to handle Phillip was just the straw that broke him? It seemed plausible, and the sooner she got away the sooner they could both get on with their lives.

"Yeah, okay," she said in this weird tone.

He tilted his head toward the bedroom she had stayed in last night, and she made her way back there. She didn't get far limping to the room though. A second later Malice had his arm wrapped around her waist and was supporting her weight as they moved forward.

"I can walk, Malice. My feet do feel better."

"You're good like this," he said gruffly and kept moving forward. "But I don't think rushing off is the best thing to do right away."

She tilted her head back and looked into his face, but he was leading her around the corner and into the room before she could say anything. "I think that is actually the *best* plan." He put Adrianna on the bed, but stayed back. He moved over to the wall and leaned his big body against it and crossed his arms. He took on this very confrontational position, but she didn't let it get to her. He was dealing with his own shit clearly, and so was she.

"What if I could get you a job in Colorado?"

That statement had everything inside of her and around her stopping. "What?" She had heard him right … right? "A job?" Adrianna shook her head in puzzlement. "You don't even know me, and I have more emotional baggage than even I can carry." To think that he would offer her a job just because he wanted to make sure she was okay had tears forming in the corners of her eyes. But of course the cynical and wary part of her, the one that had kept her alive this whole time because she relied on it, told her that this man had a lot of darkness in him, too. He might be dangerous, but underneath that tough exterior she had experienced a gentler side of him.

"Yeah, Adrianna, a job." He pushed away from the wall, and stopped when he was a few feet from her. "But before you say anything, I want you to know what you'd be getting yourself into if you agreed to it."

And there was the ball being dropped, because whatever Malice had to tell her most likely wasn't anything good.

## Chapter Six

*What in the fuck are you doing, Malice?* That was the thought that passed right through his head when told Adrianna about a job in Colorado. What the hell was he thinking offering her something that didn't even exist? And if she actually accepted the offer, even after all of the bad shit he was about to tell her, he was going to have to deal with the possible blowback from bringing an outsider to the club for protection. But he hadn't been able to help himself, and he had already said the words before he even realized what in the hell he was doing. He exhaled and ran his hand though his hair, which was getting a little too long. He grabbed the chair over by where he had just been standing and pulled it over so he could sit in front of her. For a second all he did was stare at his hands, trying to figure out what in the hell he was going to say. Did he even have a job that she could do if she agreed to come with him? He was sure he could find something for her within the club, but he would have to get it okayed by Lucien and the rest of the members. He hadn't even talked to Lucien, and although they had former pros working jobs with the MC that had nothing to do with putting out, those girls had put in their time or were recovering from a traumatic past.

But wasn't that the same thing going on with Adrianna? She was hurt and needed a safe haven. He could provide that for her. He *wanted* to provide that for her. What Malice did know with so much fucking certainty that he could have choked on that shit was the fact he couldn't let her just disappear. He didn't know why he felt that way, and didn't question it. His instincts told him she needed to stay close, and he always went with what his gut said.

"My home club is in River Run, Colorado." He looked up at her with his eyes only and kept his head downcast. "I can't say for sure what kind of job you would be doing, but it sure as fuck wouldn't have anything to do with selling your body." He straightened in his seat and rubbed his hands over the worn denim that covered his thighs. She hadn't said anything in response, but there was this very uncertain and surprised look on her face. "I know this is a really random and insane suggestion, but I'd be lying if I said that I wouldn't have a problem with leaving you at the bank to find your own way." He leaned back in the chair, and the wood creaked from his weight.

"And if I said just leave me at the bank, you would be okay with that?"

He didn't miss the way she kept picking at the edge of her shirt. At least Marx and brought in a change of clothes for her this morning. She was no longer in those near to transparent tank and shorts, and now wore a pair of these black legging type pants that formed to her like a damn second skin. At least her shirt was long and covered her ass, because he had seen the way the stretch material of her pants had molded to the big, lush mounds. The thought that every damn biker in this place would be jerking off to that sight at some point pissed him off. He lifted one shoulder in a shrug. "Totally your call. I'm not going to strap you down to my bike and make you go anywhere." No, he wouldn't, but fucking hell just thinking about watching her walk away, possibly falling into the same life she was trying to run from, had him uneasy.

"I mean, not that I won't forever be grateful that you and the others helped me, because I will be, every single day." She looked down at her hands in her lap. "I just think going with you might not be the best thing for either of us."

He wasn't going to argue how that wasn't the case, or beg her to come with him. He meant it when he said it was totally her call, and he was just going to have to deal with her decision. He stood, clenched his hands at his side, and nodded once. "If you're up to it we can leave as soon as you're ready." He might let her go, but that didn't mean he wasn't pissed because of it.

She nodded. "Yeah. I'll just finish getting ready."

He left her alone, and strode toward the front doors of the clubhouse, but stopped when he heard a door open down the hall. Looking over his shoulder, he saw Rock and Ruin come out of the back room where he knew the women they would be taking back to River Run were currently staying. There were six of them total, not a lot in the grand scheme of things, but for a town this small even one girl selling her pussy was a lot.

Rock and Ruin each lifted their chin in greeting, and the three of them headed out the main doors. Ruin was lighting a cigarette before the door even shut behind them. The sound of music blasting on the other side of the clubhouse told Malice some of the guys were working in the garage, and that was verified when there were some choice words yelled about a Harley engine.

"Everything a go for heading back to River Run tonight?" Ruin asked and moved over to one of the picnic tables off to the side.

Malice nodded. "Yeah, as long as the cargo is all set, and we don't have issues with these protesting people Marx keeps talking about." He didn't particular like referring to the women as cargo, but with all the shit happening in Fairview right now there might be prying eyes and open ears.

"It's set, just packing up some more shit, but I told them to carry light as whatever they need will be provided to them once we get back to Colorado."

Malice nodded again and leaned against the wall of the building. All he could think about was Adrianna, and what would happen to her once they left Fairview and her behind.

"Malice, man, did you hear me?" Ruin said from around his cigarette.

"What?" He could use a joint right now, something to help ease this wild tension he felt inside, but it was fucking early for all that.

Ruin inhaled deeply from his cigarette, held the smoke in, and then exhaled. "Just making sure you heard me and the shit I said about the girls?"

Malice scrubbed a hand over his face. "Yeah, I heard. I just got other things on my mind."

Rock grunted out something unintelligible, and turned to look at Malice.

"What?" Malice wasn't about to listen to Rock's bullshit either.

The other biker shrugged and moved over to sit beside Ruin on the table. "Nothing. Just wondering what's the word on that woman, and if that is what you have been focusing on lately."

"Lately? What the fuck are you talking about? We just picked her up last night." Malice knew he sounded defensive as hell.

Rock braced his arms on his thighs and stared at Malice. Rock lifted his hands in surrender. "Hey, not trying to bust your balls, man."

Malice didn't want to talk about it, because he was already feeling testy as it was because of Adrianna. "There is no word on her. I'm going to take her to the bank to get her money, and she'll be on her way." There was this awkward moment of silence, and he shook his head and shoved his hands in his pockets. "If you two have something to say, spit it the fuck out." He knew they had more on their mind by the way they looked at him, and then at each other.

"Nothing," Ruin said. "No, that's a damn lie." Ruin chuckled, but it was this deep sound that didn't hold any amusement. "I mean, you got pretty fucking territorial when Marx suggested she give it up to a john."

The sound that came from Malice had Ruin and Rock both knitting their brows. "I wasn't acting like anything. I was just pissed because it was suggested she do that shit after what had happened to her."

Rock nodded. "Yeah, that wouldn't have been my suggestion, but this is Marx's place, and we also need to remember that, Malice."

"Yeah, I didn't forget, but that doesn't mean I'm not going to stand up for a woman that was clearly hurt," Malice gritted out.

"Whoa, man, there is no need for this testy shit." Ruin held up a hand, and all amusement fled his expression.

"Besides, we both know Marx wouldn't have followed through with actually asking her if she wanted to sell her body. He may have a sick and fucked-up sense of humor, but he wouldn't further hurt a woman. He takes care of his girls just as well as we take care of ours," Rock said. "I mean he asked us to take them back to River Run so they will be safe."

Malice knew as much, but that wouldn't have changed how he acted anyway. The need to say something when that had been brought up had been fierce and strong, and if he had it to do over all over again he would have done it the exact same way. "The conversation regarding Adrianna is over."

Rock cocked a brow and lifted his hands in surrender. "Consider it ended."

They all stood there for a few moments, and although there was this heavy silence among them, it was all on Malice's end. The door beside him opened, and he looked over to see Adrianna walking out. The only thing that looked different about her was that she had put her long dark hair in a ponytail. His fingers itched as if they had a mind of their own to push away the stray piece of her bangs that blew across her forehead. She stopped, not seeing him right away, and the scent of her filled his nose. It was that same light floral aroma that had his pulse increasing, his cock hardening, and a slew of filthy fucking things slamming into his head.

"Ready?" she asked in a low voice.

Malice nodded and pushed off the wall. His t-shirt was untucked, so at least he had that going for him to hide his semi-hard cock. "Yeah, come on." He walked over to Ruin. "Let me have the van keys. I don't want her riding on the back of my bike injured like she is."

Ruin grabbed the keys out of his front pocket and handed them over.

Malice turned and gestured for Adrianna to follow him. They walked to the van, and he opened the door for her. He didn't miss the wince that covered her face, and so he wrapped his hands around her waist and gently lifted her into the seat.

"Thank you." The way she looked at him sideways, the lower half of her face partially shielded by her shoulder, made her look innocent and alluring all in the same breath.

He didn't respond, but nodded and shut the door. Making his way around the front of the van he climbed in, started the engine, and told him that leaving her like she wanted was the best thing to do ... wasn't it?

## Chapter Seven

They sat in silence as Malice drove them back into the square of town. Adrianna didn't bother trying to strike up a conversation, because her mind was focused on what her next step would be once Malice was gone and she was alone. She did think about his offer for a job, but how smart was it to go with a man she knew nothing about, was in a motorcycle club, and had told her that he would be delivering some kind of retribution to Phillip, if she hadn't already killed him? She was a wreck mentally, was emotionally unstable, and didn't think just leaving with him would solve any of the problems she currently had. But it wasn't just that. She had a lot of shit that he surely didn't need dropped in his lap. She already had enough worries and drama in her life, and getting involved in something else, even if he had been nothing but kind to her, was probably not a step in the right direction.

They finally got into town fifteen minutes later, and Malice pulled the van to a stop at the curb in front of the bank. For a moment she didn't know what to say. Did she tell him goodbye? It seemed so ungrateful to just leave this way, but it wasn't like she had a relationship with him or his club. She had known him less than twenty-four hours. Surely he had a life to get back to, maybe even had a wife or girlfriend and children? Turning so she was partially facing him, she licked her lips and saw the way he had a tight hold on the steering wheel. "Thank you so much for the ride, and for everything else." Looking away from him and out the passenger side window she saw a few people walk into the bank. "Please tell everyone else I said thank you, and if not for you and them I would probably be dead right now." She heard him grind his teeth and glanced at him again. "I tried finding the other guys to tell them thank you as well, but the inside of the club was deserted."

He was watching her, but still had that white knuckle grip on the steering wheel. "No problem. I'll let them know." He smiled, but it looked a little forced. "You sure this is what you want?"

She nodded. "I don't know if it is what I want, but it seems like the smartest thing to do right now."

He nodded. "You take care of yourself." He shifted so he could grab something out of the inside of his leather vest. It looked like a small piece of paper. He grabbed a pen from the center console and wrote something down on it before handing it over.

Adrianna held the small slip of paper in her hand and looked down at the phone number written in a masculine scrawl on it. "Your phone number." She didn't state it like a question. He would never know how much those ten digits would mean to her.

"You need anything at all just call." He nodded once more and faced the front once more.

"Thank you again." She reached out and placed her hand on his bare forearm, felt the hard muscles clench under her touch, and felt the tendrils of desire fill her. She quickly took her hand back because her desires were unwarranted and totally inappropriate given the situation. She grabbed the door handle, about to leave all of this behind her, when a sight from across the street had her stilling. Coming out of the convenience store was Phillip. He had a stark white bandage wrapped around the side of his neck, but other than that he seemed fine. Had she totally thought she hurt him far worse than she actually had? She must have, because compared to her he looked in fit condition. Her hand not holding onto the door shook slightly, but it wasn't because she was afraid of Phillip, not really. Her nerves were already shot, and seeing him walking around and laughing with the woman he was with was kind of a relief. She had worried she had killed him, and despite all the things he had done to her, and how she had fought to stay alive, having someone's death on her hands was still a heavy burden.

It seemed like the world might have stopped and gone in slow motion for as long as she stared at Phillip and the half-dressed woman he was with. But then everything came rushing back when strong fingers pressed into her jaw and she was forced to look at Malice. He wore this very concerned expression on his face. She saw his mouth moving, but there was this buzzing in her ears and she couldn't hear anything aside from that. Out of the corner of her eye she saw Phillip start to walk toward them. Although he was across the street and wouldn't be able to tell that she was in the passenger's side, or at least she hoped not, this fear that he would still be able to sense her like he was some kind of rabid animal filled her.

"Adrianna? *Christ*, what in the hell is the matter?"

Malice's deep voice finally came through the buzzing in her head, and she blinked rapidly. Not telling him that Phillip was right across the street was at the forefront of her mind, but she knew that was foolish. Malice deserved to know why she was acting like a freak. But when she looked over at the prick that was acting like she hadn't affected him in the horrifying way he had changed her, the tears from her anger burned hot in the corner of her eyes. She glanced at Malice again to answer, but she saw that his focus was on Phillip. He obviously wouldn't know who he was just by looking, but she could see how clenched his jaw was, heard the sound of his rapid, harsh breathing, and saw that he kept clenching and unclenching his hand. He knew. "Malice?"

She said his name softly, and after a few seconds he finally turned her way.

"That's him," he said between clenched teeth, but she didn't need to nod or verbally tell him that it was Phillip because she could see in his grey eyes that the knowledge was already there.

Adrianna didn't know what she expected him to do, but reaching into his cut and getting his phone out wasn't one of them. He dialed a number and put the phone to his ear. After a moment he told someone to meet them at the bank. She looked over at Phillip again and saw him going into the one and only bar in Fairview. It was barely nine in the morning, but he had always been thirsty no matter the time of day.

"Stay in the van, Adrianna," Malice said in a hard, cold voice. He looked at her again, and she swallowed roughly.

She thought he was going to climb out of the vehicle and go after Phillip, but he didn't move. "What are you going to do?"

He shook his head and focused on the bar across the street. "Nothing that doesn't need to be done."

His cryptic words had her stomach tightening. But Adrianna didn't move, and she sure as hell didn't try to get out of the van. She felt safe with Malice, and the thought of leaving that feeling and his side, especially with Phillip just across the street, was not a step she was going to take. By the time the sound of a motorcycle pierced her thoughts it had been almost twenty minutes later. The time had seemed to stand still as she sat beside Malice in this very uncomfortable silence. The man she had heard Malice call Rock pulled his bike to the curb right in front of the van. He took off his helmet, and his shaggy blond hair stood up around his hair. He had dark sunglasses on, and when he turned she could see ink coming up from under the collar of his shirt and leather vest.

"I'll be right back." Malice was out before she could even respond.

Adrianna watched him walk over to Rock, who was dismounting off his bike. They spoke too softly for her to hear what was being said even though the windows were open, but even if she hadn't seen Rock look over at the bar she knew they were speaking about Phillip. After a few minutes it wasn't Malice that came back to the van and sat in the driver's side, but Rock. She looked at him for a minute, wondering what was going on and if she should even ask. But right when she opened her mouth Rock started the engine and put the van in reverse.

"Malice has some business to take care of but will meet us back at the clubhouse."

"But my money, Phillip, and will Malice be okay—"

Rock shook his head. "Don't worry about any of that right now. I was just told to take you back to the club, and I'm not about to argue with Malice."

She was so stunned that she didn't even argue. She looked at Malice and saw that he was watching her. But he didn't stare at her long. He turned and walked across the street and right into the bar that Phillip had gone in.

****

Leaving Adrianna like that without a word on what he was doing hadn't been the classiest move, but then again Malice wasn't a classy type of guy. He acted first and thought about the repercussions later. Right now he wanted to beat the shit out of that fucking little prick that had hurt Adrianna. She might not have come out and told him that it was him across the street, but her body's reaction, and the way she looked like a deer caught in the headlights told him his answer. So, without thinking and just calling Rock over to take Adrianna back to the clubhouse, Malice had made his way to the bar.

He pulled the door open and stepped inside the dark smoky room. Some sappy country song played overhead, and although it was only a little after nine in the morning there were a few guys already at the bar with beers in front of them. Malice waited for his vision to clear, and then scanned the bar until he saw the motherfucker that was currently whispering in some skank's ear. Malice lowered his head but kept his gaze locked on the man that would soon see what it felt like to be at the mercy of someone bigger than him. Blood pumped hard and fast through him, and the testosterone and endorphins that moved through his veins made his muscles swell with the need for violence. Malice took a step forward, but when the action caused a floorboard to creak under his weight it had the patrons in the bar to stop what they were doing and stare at him as if they had just realized his presence. Just as quickly as they looked at him they turned back to their drinks. But the one person that he had all of his attention on hadn't even so much as blinked in Malice's direction.

Malice moved further into the room, and kept going until he was only a foot away from Phillip. Malice stood there for several seconds as the girl on Phillip's lap giggled and ran her fingers over the collar of his jacket. But Malice didn't move, didn't even breathe as he waited for this bastard to realize he wasn't alone. His knuckles ached from clenching his hands so tightly, and when Phillip finally looked over at him, Malice let a sadistic smile cover his face. All the things he wanted to do to this bastard played through his mind.

"What the fuck you want?" There was an almost disgusted tone in Phillip's voice, and Malice knew this guy thought he was some kind of big shit in this town. And maybe he was, but Malice didn't give a fuck either way. He didn't know Malice, but he would know soon enough what he was capable of.

Malice could have said a bunch of shit in response, but he didn't bother. This little prick would know plenty once Malice was finished with him.

Phillip pushed the woman off of his lap and slowly stood. "Is there something on your mind, asshole?"

Malice looked at the bandage that was wrapped around the side of Phillip's neck, and his already turbulent emotions went even higher. He wanted blood, wanted to break this fucker's bones, and wanted to do it all because he had dared to hurt Adrianna. "Looks like you ran into some bad luck." He didn't phrase it like a question, and when his gaze locked with Phillip's it was to see the little asshole was grinning.

"This?" He pointed to his neck, and then shrugged. "The cause of this problem will be dealt with very soon."

They stared at each other in silence for several seconds, and Malice could feel the other man's anger as if it was his own. Good, he wanted this motherfucker to be pissed, because there was no satisfaction in a fight that wasn't two-sided.

"So, unless you got something else to say instead of trying to sweet-talk me and delving into my business, I suggest you move the hell along."

Malice forced himself to relax his hands and turn around and go to the bar. He'd wait this prick out, and when he did confront him they wouldn't have an audience. The pain he delivered to Phillip would be a pleasure that rivaled all others. He rested his forearms on the scarred counter of the bar and ordered a glass of water. The mirror right in front of him reflected the numerous bottles of liquor, but also gave him an unobstructed view of Phillip. He went back to necking with the bleached blonde woman, but after a shot of whiskey and a beer to chase it down, Phillip stood and all but pulled the blonde out with him. He did glance at Malice before he left, and that had Malice's blood pumping harder and faster as his heart rate increased. Normally he just fucked someone up that needed a good ass kicking. He didn't wait and didn't care about people watching it, but this wasn't his town, and he needed to watch his step, especially with all the crap happening with the protesters and prostitutes. Pushing away from the counter and heading out, he saw Phillip get into a newer Suburban. He went over to Rock's bike, and once he had his helmet on and the engine started he pulled onto the road and followed Phillip's SUV. He didn't even care if the douche saw him following him. In fact, Phillip would have to be a fucking moron because Malice wasn't making it a secret that he was keeping on the ass of his SUV.

It didn't matter where this asshole was going, because Malice would follow him. He needed to see this guy hurt, needed to picture all the pain Adrianna had gone through in his head as he slammed his fist into Phillip's face. He continued to follow him for another five minutes. He dropped the blonde off at some broken down trailer in one of the older neighborhoods in town, and continued to drive for another ten minutes. The road became more country, and finally Phillip pulled the SUV onto the shoulder. The way he pulled the vehicle off the side of the road had the tires kicking up dust and debris. Malice pulled up behind him, cut the engine, and climbed off his bike just as Phillip opened the car door and slammed it shut.

"You fucking get up in my damn face at the bar for no apparent reason, and now you're following me?" Phillip breathed hard, and his chest rose up and down harshly. He wasn't a small guy, but compared to Malice's six-foot-three height and beefy frame he looked like an annoying gnat.

"You and I have some unfinished business that needs to be taken care of."

Phillip looked confused for a moment and then shook his head. "I don't even know who the hell you are, so you and me have no fucking unfinished business." Phillip wiped his nose, and Malice could see the guy was tweaking. His eyes were glossy, his nose red from probably doing some bumps of coke in the car, and he was twitching off and on.

"No, that is where you are wrong. We do have some shit that needs to be taken care of."

"I run this goddamn town, and if I had a beef with you I think I'd fucking know about it."

"It doesn't matter who you are in this town, or what you run." Malice ground out and took a step closer. "You did something disgusting, hurt someone that shouldn't have been touched, and now it's time you feel what it's like to get the shit kicked out of you. Maybe next time you'll think about putting your hands on a woman, especially Adrianna." Others would definitely say this was a crazy thing for Malice to do, and that taking retaliation for a woman he just met yesterday was out of left field. But the truth was he would have defended any woman that was hurt the way Adrianna was. But there was also something very delicate and innocent about her, something that had this very fierce side of him wanting to destroy anyone that thought about even coming close to her.

Phillip didn't answer, but the dark look that covered his face was confirmation enough that things were about to get dirty. "That fucking bitch had what was coming to her." He pointed to his bandaged neck. "And this shit isn't going to be forgotten, not until I show her that she needs to learn her place." Phillip reached behind him, but Malice was on him before he could get the gun that was most likely tucked in the waistband at the small of his back.

He tackled Phillip to the ground and slammed his fist into the side of his head. The sight of blood that started to pour out of his nose had Malice grinning in sick satisfaction. Before Malice could deliver another punch Phillip surprised him by head-butting him and successfully knocking him back and off of Phillip. The tangy and metallic flavor of blood filled Malice's mouth, and he turned his head and spit the shit out. He had felt his lip split, but he liked the pain. He quickly stood and saw Phillip struggling to stand. He could have easily gone after this little douche while he was out of it, but Malice wanted him to be on his feet. Once Phillip was standing, Malice charged forward. He felt all this raw energy move through him, and the image at the forefront of his mind was Adrianna, and how she had looked last night when he held her in his arms in the rain.

"You motherfucker—"

Malice stopped him from saying anything else with another land of his fist into the side of Phillip's head. The other guy stumbled back, but righted himself before he fell to the ground. The gun that he had hidden in the small of his back had fallen to the ground when Malice had first gone after him, and now he moved toward it.

*No fucking way.*

Malice was on him in the next second, and kicked the gun well out of reach. He wrapped his hand around Phillip's neck and lifted him easily off the ground. Moving forward with the other man struggling to breathe and scratching and clawing at Malice's hand, he slammed him up against a trunk of a nearby tree. He leaned in close, swore he could smell the fear that came off of Phillip, and grinned. "It's not so much fun when you're the one getting your ass kicked, is it?" He loosened his hold on his neck just slightly, and heard Phillip suck in air.

"She's just some trailer trash cunt—"

Malice cut him off by tightening his hand again. "You are one dumb fucker." He stared into the dark, beady eyes of this man that had hurt the woman Malice felt very protective over. "I'm only going to tell you this once, and believe me when I say if I ever have to repeat myself that will be the last time you are around." He leaned in another inch so they were nose-to-nose now. "You'll forget all about Adrianna if you value your life and anything you hold dear. You won't come looking for her, won't touch her, and really won't fucking think about her ever again. Understand?" He could have loosened his hold, but he didn't. It took a second for Phillip to nod, but when he did Malice reared his arm back and slammed his fist into his side. Phillip grunted, and tears formed in his eyes. "I fucking love it when grown ass men that think they are tough shit cry." Malice let him go then, and Phillip immediately dropped to the ground. "Tell me you understand what I'm saying and I may not ram my boot up your ass." Malice crouched to his haunches, and took hold of Phillip's collar, hoisting him up slightly. "Because if I have to come back here," he shook his head, "I'll bury you so damn deep no one can find you, and if they somehow did by some miracle, you wouldn't be recognizable." He hit him in the face again, this time feeling Phillip's nose break under his knuckle. Blood immediately gushed down Phillip's face, and his howl of pain and the way he curled into the fetal position had the sadistic side of Malice roaring out.

"You want her, she's yours, asshole," Phillip wheezed out, and started to choke on his own blood. There was already a bruise forming around his neck, and that really fucking pleased Malice. Of course he wanted to do a lot more damage to this little asshole, but he grabbed onto his strength and took a step back. With one more disgusted look, Malice spit out in front of Phillip the remaining blood mixed with saliva that filled his mouth. He glared at Phillip once more, and then straightened and walked to his bike. He got on and headed back to the clubhouse.

## Chapter Eight

Malice had been back at the clubhouse for a couple of hours now, and he had already finished off three beers. He didn't need to be drinking, but he was still fuming over just walking away from Phillip. He should have killed the motherfucker, because if someone had crossed his path like this any other time he would have broken their neck and not thought twice. But he had held back because Adrianna had said she didn't want any more violence, and although he might not have said he wouldn't severely hurt the bastard ex, he had held back for her. He had seen Adrianna about an hour ago, but she didn't question him on what he may or may not have done to Phillip. She was smart, and probably figured it out, but either way if she asked he wouldn't lie.

"They have just started gathering out front," Tits, one of the Fairview members, said as soon as soon as he walked inside of the clubhouse.

Malice sat next to Rock at the bar. He thought back to Adrianna, the damn obsession he was starting to have with her, and scrubbed his hand over his face. She had gone to the storage room to help Lily, one of the club whores, bring in some cases. He hadn't wanted her to go anywhere that he couldn't see her, but keeping her locked in a back room also wasn't helping her. All the shit she had been through had to be hell on a person, and he had to give her credit for the strength she showed.

"Dude, what in the hell are we going to do once she is back in River Run?" Rock asked from beside him, but kept his focus on the club pussy manning the bar. The chick had an ass on her that went on for miles. It was big and juicy, the kind Malice normally went for, but even staring at it, and knowing the front would show him a big ass set of tits, he felt no spark of arousal. He just couldn't stop thinking about Adrianna, and what would have happened if he hadn't been at the right place at the right time. She was healing, was bruised and cut up, but it would take a lot of time for her to heal on the inside.

"Dude, you fucking with me?"

He looked at Rock, who stared at him with this confused look on his face.

"I've been talking to you and you've been checking out her ass the entire time." Rocks looked over at the barmaid. "But she does have one rockin' body."

"She's yours." It wasn't like they called dibs on a woman. If they wanted them, they didn't have any trouble getting them, and the club pussy currently slinging out the drinks was no exception. Malice brought his bottle to his mouth and tipped it back. The alcohol was starting to get warm, but he didn't give a shit. His mind was preoccupied with other things anyway.

Marx came out of the backroom with a fierce and pissed off look on his face. "Those bastards are relentless," he growled out and stormed over to the front doors, but stopped before he opened them. "Tits, make sure the girls are in the back and out of the way. I don't want them around this bullshit."

Malice finished off his beer and stood. Tits was already striding back to where the prostitutes where staying, but he noticed the club pussy girls were also rounded up and ushered toward the back of the clubhouse.

"This going to get out of hand?" Rock asked from behind Malice.

Marx looked over at them. "They don't come through the gate, and thank fuck for that because I would end up killing a bastard if they did." Marx scrubbed a hand through his hair. "But they are annoying as shit, and are loud when they are spouting off their religious and judgmental bullshit." Marx turned back around and pulled the door open.

Right away they could hear the chanting of the church, and see the large group formed right on the other side of the gate that blocked off the driveway to the club.

"Get those whores out of here!"

"Dirty, filthy, and immoral sluts."

"Nothing but the devil's work behind those walls."

They kept chanting their hateful and derogatory slurs, and Malice moved closer until he was right inside of the door. He glanced behind him at the door that Adrianna and the other woman had gone behind, and no way in hell was he going to leave them to go deal with a bunch of fucking fanatics. Marx and several of the other Fairview members were standing a few feet from the gate, smokes in hand, and some holding beer bottles. They were staring at the church people, and some were getting a good laugh at them. But Malice wasn't about to tiptoe around a bunch of loons who thought that what they were doing was wrong and immoral. It was a world where people had to do what they had to do to survive. The women that sold their bodies, and looked to the clubs for protection, didn't mean they were dirty or less than anyone else. But churches like the ones right outside the gate were nothing more than cults that followed with a single-minded purpose.

One of the men that was shouting some pretty vile shit tossed a glass bottle over the gate. It barely missed some of the bikers, and that just had the whole shit-storm of violence erupting. Marx was holding one of his men back that was about ready to tear the churchgoers in two. Malice took another step forward, and the need to be with his brethren rode him hard, but he was concerned about Adrianna. And then he heard the cult going wild.

"Whores."

"Sluts."

"The devil's concubines."

He saw Adrianna and the club pussy standing off to the side by the garage. His heart started pounding fast and hard, and he moved toward her with determined, quick steps.

"You motherfucking bitch."

He stopped dead in his tracks at the deep voice that seemed to rise above the rest. He turned, and through all of the raised arms, figurative pitchforks high in the hair, and anger and hatred that swirled behind the gate, he saw that worthless prick of an ex, Phillip. His blood boiled, and he curled his hands into fists. Adrianna's ex-boyfriend was one stupid bastard, and Malice was not the type to give second warnings. He turned and made his way back to Adrianna and the other woman. They had yet to move. Adrianna wore a frightened, shocked look, and the other club woman was staring off at the crowd with this curious expression. A club pussy woman was tough—they had to be if they were going to be a part of the MC lifestyle.

"Adrianna." He called out to her, and she immediately looked his way. Her eyes widened, and she pointed out to the crowd, no doubt seeing Phillip, and hearing what he had yelled out to her. "Come here," he said at the same time he had taken a step toward her. The hairs on the back of his neck stood on end, and his gut clenched. This was a bad situation to begin with, and now with her ex here, and all the negative and dangerous energy in the air he knew it could go to a volatile level fast. He reached her in a matter of seconds, and as soon as he had his arm wrapped around her shoulder he felt her tremors start to subside

"I'm sorry. I'm so sorry." She said it like she was out of breath. "I didn't bring him here, did I?" She looked up at his face "I didn't bring this to your clubhouse, did I?"

God, he wanted to take the fear, anxiousness, and worry out of her. "No, Adrianna, you didn't do this. Those fuckers have been coming around her and stirring shit around, and that fucker…" he gritted out, trying to control himself because he was getting even more pissed by the second.

"God will judge you when you're dead, but until then we will be the jury."

Malice turned and stared at a dark haired man that stepped forward. The people around him parted, and started touching him like he was some kind of savior to them. The man wore all black, and his dark hair was slicked back from his wide brow. He wore this thick silver cross around his neck. He gripped the bars and held one hand high in the hair.

"You will be punished by the flames of hell." But the bastard smirked, and there was this glint in his eyes that made Malice feel unsteady.

"The cops have been called, but not sure how much they will be. As much as I want to open the gates and let the assholes in so they can get a whooping, I have to fucking play by the books," Marx said as he walked past them and back into the clubhouse. "I need to make sure the women are all good, but you two need to get inside." He pointed to Adrianna and the other woman.

"Gun!" The screams started right away, but the next few moments seemed to go in slow motion.

Malice turned and pulled Adrianna behind him just as Phillip pushed the cult leader aside, raised the gun high in the air, and fired off a shot. The motherfucker was smarter than Malice gave him credit for. Phillip must have put two and two together when he saw Malice's patch. And then the fucker had gotten lucky that there were these assholes outside protesting their bullshit ideals, and that Malice and Adrianna just happened to be outside, too. All this fucking chaos had helped that little prick out, but once Malice got his hands on him he was going to make sure the fucking douche never breathed again.

The fanatics scrambled away and screamed. Many people ducked, but when Phillip put his hand through the slates of the gate and pointed it right at Malice, time seemed to go to a standstill. Malice kept Adrianna behind him, and just as he went to go to the ground Phillip pulled the trigger. There was another round of screams. The cult leader was shouting some biblical stuff with his hands in the air and totally not caring that there was a shooter amongst them. It wasn't until Malice was on the ground with Adrianna underneath him that he saw the bullet slam into the concrete right beside him, and right where they had been standing.

"Get the motherfucker with the gun," Malice roared out. He wanted to go to Phillip himself, but no fucking way was he leaving Adrianna alone, even long enough that she could run into the safety of the club. He continued to shield Adrianna with his body and watched as Rock and several of the other Brothers from the charter rushed forward with their own guns held high. The cops had been called by now, and the fanatics were at least smart enough to get the fuck out of there—even their psycho leader was on the move to a car.

Phillip took off in the other direction, but right before Malice lost sight of him he ran across the street. Everything happened so fast that all Malice could do was stare in shock and sadistic pleasure as one of the church fanatics' car sped across the street and slammed right into

Phillip. That asshole flew ten fucking feet in the air before slamming down on the asphalt. Even from the distance Malice could hear Phillip's body making contact with the ground.

"Oh my God," Adrianna choked out, and then she was leaning to the side and throwing up.

Yeah, this was one of the most fucked up situations that Malice had ever been in.

\*\*\*\*

Adrianna glanced over at Malice for what felt like the tenth time in the last five minutes. It had been hours since the shooting and seeing Phillip run over by that car. It was already nightfall, the cops had come with all of their questioning, and after they had left she felt this kind of shock, but also this relief fill her. The police had said Phillip died on impact, but it was from a heart attack, and not from the actual car hitting him. Apparently he had cocaine in his system—not a surprise to her—but that upon impact his heart had already been pumping overtime, and the accident has just been that push he needed to have his heart explode—figuratively speaking. He had died of a heart attack, and not so much of the actual impact was what they told her. It was now dark out, and all she wanted to do was curl up and sleep this day away. She didn't know what the police had found out from the fanatic protestors, but right now she didn't care, and frankly didn't know if she ever would. It just went to show how fucked up this world really was.

She looked at Malice, who sat in front of her, and although she hadn't know what he had done to Phillip before that asshole had come back looking for her, she didn't care one way or another. He had saved her life once, and then did it again when he used his own body as a shield from Phillip's crazed intentions. Whatever she had felt for him before was now heightened to the nth degree, and letting him walk out of her life didn't seem like the smartest move anymore.

The silence stretched on between them, and she shifted on the bed. It might have been hours since she had been caught up in the middle of that life and death situation, but her heart still felt like it would come right through her chest. And then she'd look at Malice, and her heart would drop into her stomach.

"You're sure you're okay?" he asked again and stared at her with this very worried expression on his face.

"I am, just still a bit shocked over everything I guess."

He nodded and gave this gruff grunt of acknowledgment. "I can call the doctor in here, make sure you're okay?"

She shook her head. The bullet hadn't hit them, thank God. "No, I'm okay, really. But thank you." They sat in more silence, and the sound of their combined breathing seemed overly loud.

He had saved her, and she knew that if Phillip hadn't gotten hit by that car and died Malice would have gone after him and killed him. There had been that dangerous air about him as he held her tightly in that parking lot and made sure she was kept behind the mountain that was his body. Even now she swore she could still hear the sound of Phillip's body being hit by the car, and then slamming hard on the pavement. It was enough to make her stomach roil.

But here they were now, neither saying anything as this heavy feeling moved between them. Adrianna supposed she could have been in the main room with everyone else, but the truth was she liked being alone with Malice. He was the only one right now that made her feel safe.

"Seeing as all this shit went down, Adrianna, I can't let you just walk away," Malice said. He was hard, unyielding, and stared right at her. "I want you to come to Colorado with me. I can find you work, make sure you're safe, and most of all I want you close." He said the last part just as hard as the rest, but she heard this vulnerability in his voice that she never had before. She could still fell the anger that surrounded him from what had happened earlier. His lip was split, and she could see some bruising starting to form on his cheek and jaw. He had looked like he had gotten into a fight when he came back from town, but the bruise was from when he had taken her down to the ground to protect her.

Adrianna knew there was nothing for her in Fairview, and knew she had always planned on leaving with no set destination in mind. There wasn't anything tying her down, and many things that pushed her to follow through with what she truly wanted to do. Staring at Malice, she really didn't need to let his offer sink in. Going with him, getting a job that she could actually put herself into, work hard and make something for herself sounded very nice. But of course on the heels of that positive thought were the negative one—the wary ones—that pointed out all of the bad things that could happen. She wanted to leave, but was scared of what was out there, and especially since all of this other stuff had happened. She felt like she was walking on a tightrope and was seconds away from falling to her death. "I want to so badly, but I'm scared." Those words came from her on a whisper.

"Anyone in your situation would be scared, Adrianna. Hell, there are women out in the main room that are in tears, so what you're feeling is totally understandable."

She nodded and kept her gaze with his. "I am so glad no one was hurt, well, aside from Phillip, but I hate to say he deserved what he got."

"I hope you're not scared of me." He said it almost like an afterthought, or at least that's what it sounded like.

"I am not scared of you." Her throat felt so dry and almost like it was closing in on itself. "I'm just scared of what the next day holds, and what will happen in Colorado."

He didn't say anything for several seconds, but he also didn't look away from her. "I can understand your hesitancy, and although you don't really know me, I am glad that you feel safe with me." He ran his palms up and down his thighs, and she couldn't help but watch the way his biceps and forearms flexed. "If I had to do all of this over again, I would, Adrianna, in a fucking heartbeat."

She felt her pulse race at his words. There was so much heart and determination in them that she didn't doubt the sincerity of what he said. "I can never thank you enough." They stayed silent. It could be dangerous leaving with him, but honestly it couldn't be much worse than what she had lived with. Look at how things had played out in the last twenty-four hours. She hadn't realized she was looking at her feet until she lifted her gaze and stared at Malice again. He seemed to be the master at not showing his emotions or what he might be thinking. She on the other hand didn't even try hiding how she felt. "Okay." She saw the way his shoulders relaxed as if he had been tense.

He nodded. "Good. I'm glad, because believe me when I say I think this is the smartest and safest move."

Maybe she wasn't as strong and independent as others out there, and feared what the world held, but she liked to think of herself as strong in her own right. She had survived, and wasn't that what mattered? Before she could respond to what Malice had said he started speaking again.

"We'll leave in the next few hours. Once we get to River Run I'll have you stay at the clubhouse since I'd rather you do that than stay in a hotel. It's safer, too, and I want you close."

She smiled at the last part he said. Her throat clogged from emotion, anticipation, and of course a little bit of fear of the unknown.

"I'll need to talk all of this over with my club seeing as you're an outsider."

"Do you think they will be okay with me staying there?"

"I'm not about to back down if they aren't." Again, he said that last part hard and unyielding. "Tomorrow we can get you situated at a different place, and we can talk about that job. Sound good?" He said the last part a little more gently and even offered a small smile.

"Okay." Her palms were sweaty, her heart rate picked up pace, and she actually thought she might pass out from the information overload and everything that seemed to be falling into her lap. Malice stood and turned, but before he could leave she called out. "Malice?"

He stopped and turned around.

"Thank you so much for being there." It was like this heavy silence filled the room.

"You're welcome, Adrianna." He said her name so softly, so gently, that even after all of this she felt the tendrils of desire move through her.

And then he left her alone in the room, and all she did was think about what would happen in the future. Things couldn't get any worse, right?

****

The ride to River Run had been long, but Adrianna had fallen asleep for the majority of it. She didn't even think it was possible to sleep after all the shit that happened, and with the adrenaline that was a steady flow through her, but once she closed her eyes she had been out. Thank God those protestor people hadn't been waiting for them when they left, because that was the last thing they needed right now. But if they were smart they would keep low given the fact they had rundown someone in their haste to escape. With six other women in the van it was a bit crowded, but with Malice driving instead of riding on his Harley with the other two guys, he had insisted she ride up front with him. She didn't know any of the details about why they had a van full of women, and frankly didn't want to know. But given the fact on how they were dress—like they were selling their bodies—and the fact she heard some of the hateful things those protestors were saying.

She put everything else to the back of her mind and just focused on what concerned her. She was awake now and watched the large cabin-like compound come into view. It resembled a lodge, and Malice pulled the van up to a gate and waited for two guys to open it for him. Malice then drove the van up the unpaved dirt road. She couldn't help the way her belly tightened and her heart raced the closer they got. This was a totally new experience, and she was doing it with a man she hardly knew, but one she realized she felt more comfortable with than anyone else in her life. But for as strange as all of this was she felt that it was the right thing for her to do. Besides, it couldn't be any worse, right?

Malice pulled the van to a stop in front of the cabin and cut the engine. It was still dark out, but the sun would be rising soon. Adrianna felt dirty and gritty from

being in that car for so many hours, and from not
bothering to shower after the Phillip and cop situation.
Sleep sounded much better right now than getting cleaned
up anyway. Besides, she was curious to see what this
place looked like on the inside, and was nervous to see
how Malice's friends and the members of his club
thought of her staying there. Before she could exit the car
there were a few bikers coming out of the front doors of
the cabin. They looked just as intimidating as Malice, and
the closer they got she noticed the patches they wore on
their leather vests. Of course they all said The Brothers of
Menace MC, but the two men that were in front of the
other bikers had patches that read PRESIDENT and V.
PRESIDENT stitched into the chest part of their cuts.

"That's Lucien, our club's president, and Kink,
the VP."

She turned and looked at Malice.

"Don't worry. They look meaner than they
actually are." Malice smiled, but even Adrianna could tell
that his words weren't entirely true.

The one named Lucien opened up the back door
and the girls got out. There were a few low murmured
words from the bikers and then responses from the
women. But Adrianna hadn't been able to really gauge
what was going on by what they said. When the last
woman was out Adrianna glanced over her shoulder and
locked gazes with Lucien. He was a big man, just as big
and imposing as Malice. His hair was short and dark, and
he had these eerie silver colored eyes that made her feel
like he knew what others were thinking without anyone
saying anything.

"The trip went off without any more shit
happening?" Lucien asked.

"Surprisingly, yeah."

She looked over at Malice after he had spoken, and she could see he was now tense when just moments before he had been relaxed. He had since moved to the passenger side of the door, and before she could roll down the window, Lucien had her door opened. The breeze blew by her face, rustling her hair and bringing the scent of booze, marijuana, and motor oil.

"And you're good?" Lucien asked her.

She looked at him, and nodded. There was a very dangerous air around him that seemed charged with this deadliness. Malice was the same way, but she couldn't quite explain why she felt so comfortable with Malice and not this man. "Yes, for the most part. Thank you." Adrianna didn't miss how he scanned her face with his gaze, and then looked at her neck. She knew how she appeared, knew the bruising and marks on her face and throat were nasty and telling.

Lucien didn't say anything else to her, and lifted his gaze to Malice, who still sat right beside her. "Once everyone is settled in and had some rest we need a meeting." There was this cryptic quality to Lucien's voice.

Malice didn't verbally respond, just nodded, and then Lucien did the same. She saw the way Malice still had his hands on the steering wheel, and how tightly his hands were clenched around it. Lucien left her door open and turned to walk back into the cabin where the rest of the men and women had gone. The silence descended upon them, but this wasn't the comfortable kind they had shared before.

"You can rest up here for the time being, but I am going to look for other accommodations for you." He turned and looked at her. "You're safe here, and no one will hurt you."

"Okay, thank you." She looked over at the cabin again. "Just as long as it isn't an inconvenience to anyone—" Before she could finish her sentence Malice had a hold of her hand. Adrianna glanced down at where he had his much larger hand over hers, and then looked at his face.

"It isn't an inconvenience, and if I didn't want you here I wouldn't have even suggested it, Adrianna." There was this hard, angry edge to his voice.

"Okay." That was all she could say. She knew that her attitude was timid and standoffish, but this whole situation was different from what she had ever known. Someone was going out of their way to make sure she was safe. Maybe it was her being a doormat, or not standing up for herself and thinking more highly of what others were doing? She might not be able to fully express how much all of this meant to her, but it meant the world. "Malice?"

He was still holding her hand, and now ran his thumb along the back of hers. He didn't answer, but looked up at her.

"Thank you for helping a total stranger." She might be saying "Thank you" a lot, but she would keep saying it. She really was grateful. She felt the heat in the van increase and felt perspiration start to dot the area between her breasts.

"You don't have to keep thanking me, Adrianna."

"I know, and I'm sure you're getting sick of hearing it, but I've never had anyone do the things you've done for me." Whatever was happening right now was intense and potent. She felt the hairs on her arms stand on end, felt everything inside of her race to the surface and heat her skin. They continued to stare at each other, and even with the shadows of darkness moving through the interior of the vehicle, Adrianna could clearly see the way his pupils dilated. This need to open up to Malice moved through her and filled her in a comforting, *real* way. As strange as it sounded, it really did feel like there was this magnet pulling her toward him in the literal and figurative sense. Adrianna had never believed in happily-ever-afters, never thought soul mates or true love were real. And although she still didn't know if she believed in those things, she did have faith in what was real and right in front of her. Malice was those two things, and she knew she wasn't the only one that felt this connection either.

Slowly, they both started to move closer, and it was like this cord was being tightened. Her breathing increased, and Malice's chest rose up and down, hard and fast. God, she had never met a man that was so ruggedly masculine, and so intoxicating that she felt this growth of life spring up inside of her just from being in his presence.

When there was only an inch between them she had to force herself to keep her eyes open as arousal pounded through her veins like an angry drum. She was wet between her legs, and there was no doubt that her nipples were pressing against the material of her shirt. "Malice, do you feel this, too?" She could have kicked herself for saying out loud what was supposed to be an inner thought. But he didn't respond and instead groaned deeply, took his other hand and gripped her chin between his thumb and forefinger, and held her in an unmovable hold. And then his lips were on hers, and he stroked his tongue along the seam of her mouth. A gasp left Adrianna on its own, and Malice took that time to delve his tongue inside of her mouth, and fuck her like she wanted him to do between her thighs. That thought and filthy image slammed into her head and made it spin with desire.

It was clear he was being gentle with her as he held her chin between his fingers. But the sting from her tender lip speared through her, and a gasp of pain left her. Malice pulled away instantly, and lowered his gaze so he was looking at her lip.

"Fuck, I'm sorry." He still hadn't moved away from her, and his minty breath from the gum he had been chewing moved along her face.

"Why?" She breathed that word out.

"You're hurt, and I shouldn't have been so forceful. I shouldn't have even kissed you." He went to pull away, but as if on instinct she reached out and placed her hand over his that was still holding onto her chin. He stilled, glanced into her eyes with his gaze, and she swore he stopped breathing.

"I don't want you to stop." Licking her lips and feeling the tender spot on her mouth, she wanted him kissing her again so that discomfort could be erased with how good he made her feel. Malice leaned in close and pressed his mouth to the corner of hers. The kiss was gentle, comforting, and not at all how it had been just seconds before—how she actually wanted it. He pulled away far too quickly, but she knew it was for the best. This was not the time or place for any of this, and although she didn't want to let go of these feelings moving through her, or away from Malice for that matter, things *were* moving so fast.

He let go of her chin and shifted in his seat so he was facing out the front windshield. "I'm sorry about that again." When he ran his hand over his hair and breathed out, she felt very uncomfortable. Of course she didn't want him to be sorry for what they had done, because she wasn't.

He looked at her then, and she saw the way his throat worked as he swallowed. "But I'm not sorry you did it, or that I really enjoyed it." They stared at each other for several seconds, and then he breathed out and climbed out of the van. She sat there alone and in silence, watching him through the front windshield as he walked around the front of the vehicle and stopped at the passenger side. Grabbing the handle and twisting it, she pushed it open before he could, because she knew that was what he had been going to do. Malice wrapped his hands around her waist when she went to climb down, and easily lifted her off the seat and set her on the ground. For a second he kept his hands on her, and stared down at her with this half-lidded, barely restrained look on his face.

"After we have rested up we can talk about that job and where you can stay until you get on your feet."

Talking wasn't what she wanted to do, but she nodded regardless. In fact, she was still aroused, even though he had gotten cold so quickly.

"Come on. You have to be beat." He turned and stared walking forward the front of the cabin, and she had no choice but to follow. Even after everything that had happened, and the sudden arousal and awkwardness, Adrianna knew that this was still the best choice she had made. At least that was what she kept telling herself. Even though she felt this very good sensation because she was moving on with her life, she also knew that jumping into all of this with both feet and her eyes closed could very well end in disaster.

## Chapter Nine

Kink pulled his Harley into Sarah's driveway, cut the engine, and willed himself to calm down. The last thing he wanted to do was piss her off, because she was a mega bitch as it was, and he was willing to talk this out with her instead of going ballistic like he wanted to. Taking off his helmet and hanging it from his handle, Kink sat there for a moment and stared at the small ranch style house on the outskirts of River Run. He thought about the conversation he'd had with her a few days ago, the one that had sent him into a ballistic rage and had him taking out three guys before Lucien stepped in and told him to take it easy. It wasn't just about kicking those fuckers' asses, but making money for The Brothers. Those bare knuckle fights might have helped relieve his anger and tension, but it didn't help his MC if no one bet against him. He pushed those thoughts out of his mind and made his way toward Sarah's front door. He hadn't called and told her he was coming over, because the cold hearted bitch would probably leave just so he couldn't see Callie. Seeing his kid every other weekend and once a week was a load of horseshit, but he had toed the line and kept straight with the agreement. Seeing her those few days a month was better than nothing at all.

Once in front of the door he brought his closed fist down on it three times. He was still pissed, and being here, so close to Sarah—the woman trying to keep him from his child—didn't help his anger. He was about to pound on the door again when it swung open. Sarah stood on the other side, her clothing looking like she was heading out to the strip club to make a few bucks. But then again that was where he met her out, where he'd fucked her, and what her entire life had been about.

"What in the hell are you doing here?" She leaned against the frame, her willowy frame doing nothing now but making his balls crawl into his body.

"Who is it, Sarah?"

Her douche ass boyfriend called out, and it took everything in Kink not to holler out for the fucker to come out and start shit with him in person.

"Dale, just go back to watching your show." She stared at him with this fucked-up look on her face. "Seriously, you know you can't just come all up in here without talking to me first. I should call my attorney and let him know the stunt you're pulling." She smiled smugly. "Guarantee that will ensure me moving to California is in the best interest for Callie."

He breathed in and then breathed out, reining in his anger and annoyance for the mother of his kid. "Yes, Sarah, I should have called first," he gritted out, "but you and me both know you wouldn't have answered. I needed to talk to you, to try and work this out."

She didn't respond.

"Waiting those few months for Callie to turn eighteen isn't going to fuck with your goddamn happiness. What you are doing is selfish." Kink was not the type of man to work out his problems with conversation. He took what he wanted when he wanted, and didn't give two shits about the outcome as long as it was in his favor or in the favor of the MC.

"Listen, when she turns eighteen she can do whatever the hell she wants to do. Hell, good riddance. If she wants to talk to a judge after I get the all clear to go," she shrugged, "she can do that, too. It'll take her a long time to speak to someone in River Run about getting emancipated if that's what she wants. I'm not an expert in the legal system, but I know the rules of this town and what my lawyer drafted up during the custody hearing, and what you signed." She gripped the door, intent on shutting it. "That's it, Kink, okay?"

"Dad?"

He glanced over Sarah's shoulder and saw Callie standing at the top of the stairs. She looked worried, and he hated that she was feeling that way over all this shit going on. "It's all right, baby."

She made her way downstairs, and he felt his anger fade—slightly. When Sarah stepped in front of his vision of Callie he glowered at her and forced himself, once again because she knew how to fucking push his buttons, to remain calm. "Clearly this isn't going to work out, Sarah, but I told you on the phone once that you're not talking my fucking kid. I'll be contacting my lawyer as well." He didn't know shit about legal standings, but he had a feeling she was blowing smoke up his ass. No way in hell did she get all of this approved right from under him, and in such a short time. He also had this sick feeling that she assumed he'd roll over and do what she said so not to rock the boat, but she clearly didn't know him very well. He noticed the way her smug expression morphed marginally to annoyance and then worry. Yeah, the bitch was crazy, and he'd bet his left nut that her real plans were to hightail it out of her with her POS boyfriend right from under his nose.

"You want your daughter to go through the trauma of a court hearing, of having to talk to a judge and all that?" She was grasping at straws, that much was clear.

"Using guilt to make me back down isn't going to work. I didn't get a notification from my lawyer about any of this shit, but clearly trying to work this out with you on an adult level isn't going to work. I'm not a genius in law, Sarah, but I know enough that you can't just up and move to another state." He had been so livid after talking to her earlier in the week that all he could think of was trying and talking to her about it all. And then when he cooled off enough that he realized that none of this even sounded right, and that she might make a run for it—even if it was illegal on so many levels—pissed him off even more. Douche-bag came out from the living room, looking good and drunk with a beer in hand and smelling like he hadn't showered in a week. Kink curled his lip in disgust.

"Hey, get the fuck off my doorstep, asshole."

Kink turned and looked at the fucker that was half his size and sporting a beer gut. "You better shut your old man up, Sarah." He spoke to her but kept his gaze trained on her boyfriend.

"Dale has every right to be here. Once we get married he'll be Callie's stepfather."

"Oh hell no," Callie said from the stairs.

Yup, she was his daughter all right. That had him grinning.

"Callie, shut up and let the grown-ups talk."

Fuck. No. "Callie, baby girl, head up on stairs, please." He kept his voice low and his focus trained on Dale. He saw Callie head back upstairs through the corner of his eye, and once she was gone he reached out and gripped Dale's collar. Lifting him easily off the ground Kink yanked him closer until they were nose to nose. "You ever talk to my daughter that way again and I'll rip your motherfucking balls off and roast them on my grill."

"Kink, get out of here before I call the cops," Sarah said in a slightly wavering, but still high pitched voice.

Kink stared at Dale right in the eyes for a few more seconds, and then tossed him aside as if he were a bag of potatoes. "You don't want to fuck with me, Sarah, because I will bring the wrath of The Brothers of Menace down on your ass." With that he turned and stormed back to his bike. Once on it with his helmet on his head, he glanced up at one of the second floor windows. He saw Callie standing there, and it broke his damn heart having to leave her. She blew him a kiss goodbye, and after a lift of his hand to tell her he was leaving, he cranked the engine and pulled out of the driveway. He was even more feral then he had been when all this shit started. What he needed was a good, hard drink, maybe a fight, and a fierce hard fuck to get his mind off of the shit-storm that was currently his life.

An hour later and he was at the bar, good and drunk, and playing darts with Rock. The other biker had already been at the local Brothers bar in River Run. Kink threw back another shot, but there was no burn from the harsh, but smooth flow of the alcohol. His throat was numb, his vision was blurry, and he was wearing a thick frame of beer goggles.

He turned toward the bar and slammed the shot glass on the counter. "Another shot of Jack."

"Kink, dude, how about we call it a night, or at least go back to the club and drink there?" Rock said right behind him.

He turned only his head and glanced at the other Brother. "Why, because I'm kicking your ass at darts?" He cocked a brow, knowing that he had slurred those words out, but wanting to be so drunk that he couldn't even walk let alone speak.

"In your dreams, asshole," Rock said through a grin. "But you're drunker than piss right now, and I know how this will end if you keep slugging them shots back." When Kink didn't respond, just stared at Rock, the other man continued. "You're going to get in a fight and fuck someone up, the cops will be called, and then I'll have to bail your ass out of jail."

Kink shook his head and snorted at that thought. "Yeah, that will probably be the outcome tonight."

"Hey, baby."

He turned to his right and saw one of the bar flies that frequented this place regularly.

"You wanna take me home tonight?"

She had been rubbing up on him for the last hour, but he hadn't nearly been drunk enough to take her slutty ass home. Now though? Now he was good and wasted and she looked like she could handle one hell of a pounding. The bartender set another shot down in front of him, and he glanced at Rock, who still stood toward his left. But Rock wasn't bitching about him drinking and starting a fight, and instead was busy picking up the young waitress. Kink grabbed his shot and tossed it back, and when he slammed the glass on the counter for a second time the skank rubbed her tits up against the side of his arm.

"Come on, Shuga, take me back to your place and show me how a real man fucks his woman."

He pushed her away enough that he could turn and stare at her face on. "You're not my woman." He continued to stare at her. The make-up she had one was thick and looked suffocating, and her fake ass eyelashes made her look like she should be standing on the corner of Colfax. But she had a good body, didn't smell like booze or stale cigarettes like the rest of the women at the bar did, and he needed to fuck tonight. "You're just a body I'm going to use to get off tonight." He wanted her to know exactly what this was between them, and make no mistake that there would be anything more than a few hours of hot, sweaty sex involved. She was silent for several seconds, and he could see the sliver of her anger at his coarseness, but he knew she would still go home with him. She was the type of woman that was desperate for attention, and he was willing to give her that attention, but only on his terms.

"Whatever you need, baby." She lifted her arm and ran her hand over his cut.

He grabbed her wrist in a loose, but secure hold. "Don't fucking touch the leather."

She took her hand from his hold and cradled it to her chest. He knew he hadn't hurt her, and if she wasn't used to his type of breed of male than she could turn her ass around and find a pansy ass drunk that was loitering around. They stared at each other for several seconds, and then she plastered on a smile he was sure got her a lot of shit from these lowlifes that surrounded them.

"I'm ready when you are."

It would take him a minute to get hard once he had her back at his place, thanks to the alcohol and the fact she was a butterface, but he'd deal with it. Right now he just needed to lose himself in a warm, female body, and forget about all the negative shit surrounding his life.

## Chapter Ten

Malice sat around the meeting table of The Brothers of Menace. All of the members were in attendance: Lucien their President, Kink the VP, Tuck, Ruin, and Rock. Malice had gotten back five hours ago. It was the middle of the day, but Adrianna and the women were still sleeping. They needed that rest though after the last day and a half of fucked-up shit that had happened. Ruin and Rock looked worse for wear, and Malice knew he probably looked the same way. He hadn't gotten more than a few hours of sleep before he was wide awake and staring at the ceiling thinking about Adrianna and the feel of her lips on his, and then having this meeting with the club. He wanted to get this meeting over with anyway. Lucien might have known he was bringing Adrianna with him, knew about the shooting and Phillip getting it, but that didn't mean the President was good with it all. For one thing this brought a lot of attention to the club, and not in a good way. They wanted to be on the down low, and having this shit that had made the papers in Utah was not the kind of attention they needed. They already had a bad reputation as it was. This might have all happened because he brought Adrianna into the club, but he wouldn't have changed it, and he'd deal with the repercussions.

"Okay, so we know why you brought her back to Fairview's clubhouse, but tell me again why you brought her here." Lucien leaned back in his leather chair, and it creaked from his weight. The silence that filled the room was because everyone was focused right on Malice, waiting to see why he had acted so out of character.

He took on the same relaxed position as Lucien. "I've told you I couldn't leave her there with all that shit that happened with her ex, and sending her on her way was not something I felt comfortable with."

Lucien nodded. "I know, but that is not what I meant. You have never given two shits about what happens to a woman once you've had her."

"I didn't *have* her." He growled out at his president, not meaning to show disrespect, but no one was going to imply Adrianna was something she wasn't. "I just feel protective of her."

"Okay, but that doesn't really answer what I was asking."

Yeah, Malice fucking knew that. "Because leaving a hurt woman like that isn't my style. And last I checked it isn't The Brothers' style either. We save women when it calls for it. We aren't bastards all the time." He had no issues beating the shit out of a man for club business or out of retaliation, just like he had done with Phillip, but Malice also didn't tell Lucien that he cared for Adrianna more than he probably should. He stared at the president, and the expression on his face told Malice that Lucien was holding onto his own irritation and anger over the situation.

"You want to fuck her or something? Even beat up she's a hot piece of ass," Kink said.

Kink might be the VP of the club, but that didn't stop Malice from turning a nasty glare his way.

"You better watch your fucking mouth, Kink."

There was a stoic expression on the other man's face. He looked hung-over, as did the rest of the members that hadn't gone on the run, but Kink looked a little darker than normal, and it was clear the member had some shit he was dealing with. But Malice didn't care because they were all dealing with their own problems, and just because they were in a bad place didn't mean that kind of shit needed to be said.

Kink's short brown hair was in his ever-present faux hawk, and there were dark circles under his light blue eyes. Malice could also see the tattoos that covered his chest and neck as they moved out from the collar of his shirt.

"Damn, testy much?" Kink asked with a smart assed smirk covering his face.

"Yeah, when you are clearly running your mouth on things you know nothing about." Malice growled out the words, and the sound of the other members shifting in their seats as the tension increased filled the air around him.

"All right, that's enough, Kink and Malice," Lucien said in his booming voice. He leaned forward and folded his hands together on the tabletop. The members of The Brothers of Menace ranged in age from forty to fifty, and although Lucien was only forty-two years old the weight of being a MC President clearly showed on his face. He was tired, but then again they all were.

"All I'm saying is that Malice should tell it like it is, and not try and justify his real intentions with a bullshit excuse," Kink said, clearly ignoring his and Lucien's warning that he needed to shit the fuck up.

"Christ, Kink, just shut the hell up," Lucie roared out. "We are all going through our own shit right now."

For several seconds no one said anything, but Malice did look around the table at each member. There was clear curiosity in their expressions over what Kink had said, but he couldn't blame them. Aside from Molly he didn't bother with feelings and emotions, and sure as fuck didn't bring women back to the club. He knew he was throwing off some proprietary vibes, but he didn't give a shit.

"I wasn't about to leave her there bloody and beaten, and passed the fuck out, and besides, I feel something more for her, and I'm not going to let that just go."

"Okay, good, now we are getting somewhere. Besides, I wouldn't have wanted you to do a fucked up thing like leave her behind either," Lucien said.

"I took her back to Marx's place, and their doc checked her out." He heard Marx's words play through his head again—even if he had been busting balls—it still pissed Malice the fuck off. "I had every intention of letting her go on her way the next morning, but I ran into the guy who used her as a human punching bag." This was all being repeated for the rest of the members because Lucien knew all of this already. "And then you know the rest about the fucking fanatics, and that motherfucker getting hit by the car." Malice glanced at Kink, and although he didn't have any problems with any of the other members, he was still fuming over the comments the VP had made.

"Finish, Malice." Clearly Lucien could see that he was on the edge.

"She has no one, and was planning on leaving Fairview with a couple hundred dollars, but I feel very protective of her, like I said, and I wanted her hear at the safety of the club." He was staring at the President again. There was more silence, a few clearings of throats, and Malice knew he was starting to show his anger and emotions for this girl.

"And so you thought it was good to bring her to the clubhouse when she is an outsider and not your old lady?" Again, Kink was the one to speak.

"What the fuck difference does it make? We helped out the prostitutes in Denver, even fucking bought the cabin for them so they could heal. I didn't think we were a bunch of lowlife bikers like everyone in town claims we are, but maybe one of us is." He clenched his jaw and curled his hands into fists. Malice got along with everyone, but he was on edge over this whole Adrianna situation, and things hadn't worked out any better when Kink thought it was cool to run his fucking mouth. But now both of their testosterone and rage were rising, and he knew that things would get really ugly and fast if this kept up.

"What the fuck is up with you anyway? You've had a stick up your ass since you got back," Kink growled out.

"What the fuck is *my* problem?" Malice slowly shook his head and felt his blood start to boil.

"Yeah. All I asked was if you wanted to fuck her, and you freaked out. Maybe you're pissed because she doesn't want to fuck *you*."

Malice stood so fast his chair skidded back and slammed into the wall. Kink stayed in his seat, looking unaffected although Malice could see the other man was tense all over.

"Sit down, Malice," Kink gritted out. "You don't want to do this when clearly your head is all messed up."

Malice opened his mouth, but Lucien slammed his fist on the table.

"Malice, sit the fuck down. Kink, shut the fuck up."

It took Malice a minute, but he finally sat down and reined in his temper. Shit, he was losing it and with one of his brothers. He ran a hand over his face, felt the trimmed hair of his bead scrape along his palm, and sighed. He needed a drink, and maybe a joint, but first he'd get this shit straightened out.

"Calm the fuck down, and just tell me what your plan is with this woman," Lucien gritted out, and it was clear he was trying to calm himself down. "If you want her for your old lady then you better own up to that shit right here, right now."

Malice never let anyone talk to him like that, even a Brother, but this was the prez, and he respected the hell out of Lucien.

"Because you know unless a woman is an old lady, cooking, cleaning, or fucking, we don't let pussy stay around here for nothin'."

Malice let out a deep, hostile sound.

"Chill. I am not implying she should be club pussy, but those women out there chose to be here. They like this life, and even want it. You want Adrianna then, just say so and all of this will be settled, man. "

Malice and leaned back in his chair. There was definite tension in the room still, but not just from him and Kink. The rest of the members were feeling it, too. They were a family, and when they started going after each other it wasn't good for anyone. He looked at each of the men once more, his family, his brothers, and his club. He then thought about Adrianna and what he really wanted from her. Malice didn't care that it had only been a couple of days since he found her and she had been in his life. He had experienced a hell of a lot with her in that short time. He looked at Kink, stared at the asshole that had pissed him off royally, and then looked at Lucien. "Yeah, I want her as my old lady."

Lucien didn't respond right away, but finally he nodded. "Okay, glad you owned up to it, brother. Now, let's just move on from this."

"Sounds good," Malice said in a low voice.

Damn, he had just met her, but he had claimed her as his old lady in front of his club. That was some serious shit, and he hadn't even talked to her about it. Claiming a woman as an old lady was major shit, and Malice had already been down that road with Molly. He never thought he would need or want another woman like that, but he also couldn't deny that he felt something strong and real for Adrianna. It wasn't like anything he had felt with Molly, and that was some hard-core scary shit given the life he led. "I want to bring another matter up. I want to talk about Adrianna working and staying in the house with the other women. I think she could help out, and it would allow her to get on her feet. But this would be temporary as I want to make sure things are settled for her before I even bring the old lady business up with her." Lucien lifted his brow once again. "You want her working where the pussy for sale is at?"

Malice knew what Lucien was getting at.

"I don't want her there to spread her legs. But we don't have johns going to the cabin, and those women are all trying to heal, too." He forced the words out and felt his jaw lock up as he clenched it hard. He reminded himself to calm down because this was his President, but just the thought of any other man touching Adrianna had this murderous rage moving through him.

Lucien held up his hands. "I'm just surprised that was where you wanted her to stay. I thought maybe you'd just put her up at your place or even at the motel."

Malice shook his head before Lucien even finished. "No. I don't want her at some motel, and I'm only ever home when I have Dakota. I want to make sure she is comfortable with me and this situation before I bring up her moving in with me. If she isn't staying at the club, the next safest and most logical place for her to be is at the cabin."

He placed a hand on the table and drummed his fingers on the wood. "This would have to be brought to the table for a vote as this would mean taking her on as an employee ... kind of"

Malice nodded. He had been with the Brothers for a long ass time, and although they had all been Nomads at one time before they created this charter and moved to River Run several months back, they were still a part of The Brothers of Menace MC. They made their living selling pussy. That wasn't a secret, but the women that worked for them were consenting and had chosen this as the path they wanted to take with their lives. They offered them protection, made sure they got whatever they needed, and even had a large cabin built on secluded acres for them. Over the past several months they had taken on battered women that had sold themselves in Denver and had been beaten up by their pimp. They built a home for them so they could recoup and get on their feet, and taken the financial hit for having to do that. But for every violent and illegal thing The Brothers of Menace did they reciprocated that with something that could help someone else.

"I think it would be good for the other women to have her around, especially since she has experienced what they have." Rock was the one to speak.

Everyone glanced at him.

He shrugged. "What? I can't put an insightful comment in here?" He grinned. "We probably could have thought this situation out better, no arguments there, but what's done is done." No one said anything, and the tension eased.

"Okay, I'm ready to put this thing to bed, because everything has been laid out flat and things are looking like they are going where they need to." Lucien glanced at Malice and then looked at Rock. "I for one can say I'm glad that piece of shit got what came to him. Hurting a woman is grounds for a broken neck in my books."

There was a round of grunts as the members agreed. "The vote is for Malice's woman to stay at the cabin and help out with whatever needs to be done at the cabin until she gets on her feet and heals." He looked at Malice and nodded. "That about right?"

"Yeah." But the thing was Malice didn't know what would happen once she was healed and "on her feet". Could he let her go? After the fear and worry he felt when they were back in Fairview ... no, he wanted her, had already declared that, and he was going to have to show her that staying by his side was a hell of a lot better than being on her own.

"You know the drill. Yea or nay." Lucien gave his yea vote and started with Malice. Of course his vote was yea. Then it went on down the line with Tuck, Ruin, Rock, and stopped on Kink. He stared at the other biker, and although they had gotten into it just moments before, they were still family, and things would eventually smooth out. There was clearly something going on with Kink, though.

"Yea."

"Good, a unanimous vote." Lucien tilted his chin toward him. "Malice, I want you, Tuck, and Ruin to finish this run by taking the girls over to the cabin tomorrow morning. Rock, stay here and make sure shit's good with the Fairview charter. With everything that happened there I want to make sure they are holding up and don't need extra muscle."

Rock nodded.

"Hopefully things start to settle back to normal." Lucien glanced around the table. "Any other business that needs discussed since we are all gathered?"

There was a collective grunt, and everyone murmured "no". Once that was said everyone stood and left the room. Malice did the same and walked over to the bar and ordered himself a double shot. He glanced down at the scarred bar and saw some pamphlets. Once he had one opened it and scanned the interior his blood ran cold.

"Who the fuck brought these in here?" Malice yelled to be heard over the music and voices.

Pierce, a prospect, came over to him. "I did. They were shoved in the mailbox by the gate. Thought some of these fuckers could use some religion."

Malice looked at the pamphlet again, saw that it was from The Church of the Good and Only in Fairview, Utah, and set it back on the bar. Had that cult followed them all the way from Utah? It seemed pretty fucking ridiculous, but the proof was right in front of him. "Well, shit." He scrubbed a hand over his face and breathed out. It could be nothing at all, just a member from that fucked-up cult trying to scare them, but he'd make sure everyone was on alert. He got everyone's attention, and relayed what he just found out. "It could just be one of them tying to fuck with us, but I want everyone to know so they can be on the lookout."

Everyone murmured their agreement. The cult hadn't done anything but be annoying in their picketing at Fairview, but Malice didn't put anything past a group of people that were intent on making their twisted and warped beliefs a reality.

Everyone went back to doing what they were doing, and Malice leaned against the bar again. It was still light outside, but dusk would be approaching soon, and after the last couple of days he had been through a drink was in order. He threw the shot back, and glanced to his left and at the hallway. He could just barely see the room that he had set Adrianna up in. The other women were upstairs, and maybe it was foolish of him, but the room he had put Adrianna in was his. Bracing his elbows on the bar he closed his eyes, feeling his exhaustion finally take hold.

Someone clapped him on the shoulder, and he opened his eyes and turned to see Tuck standing beside him. "Shit, man, things got hot and heavy back there with you and Kink."

Malice nodded, but didn't look over his shoulder to see where he knew Kink was standing. "Yeah, not sure what is up his ass, but I didn't have to get all pissed like that either." He rubbed his eyes.

"I'm not sure what the hell is going on with him, but I do know he went over to see his ex-old lady and his daughter, and when he came back he was in a foul mood."

Malice shook his head. Great, what the club needed was more drama. "Lucien talk to him?" He turned his head and glanced at Tuck. The light that came through the window slashed across his scar.

"Yeah, and it calmed his ass down a bit, but he has been drinking non-stop, and refuses to talk to anyone about whatever the issue is. But we all know that if there is an issue we are all here for him. It's up to Kink if he wants to open up and unload his emotional baggage."

Yeah, that was the good thing about being in the MC and having a permanent family. Tuck stayed for a few more minutes, tossed back a shot with him, and then headed toward the back of the club and to his room. Malice stayed there for another few minutes, and when he turned to head back and crash for another few hours in one of the extra rooms, Lucien moved over to him.

"You got a minute, brother?"

"Yeah, I was just going to get another hour or two of sleep since I didn't get much."

Lucien nodded. "I won't take much of your time then." He tilted his head toward the rear entrance. They moved toward it, and once they rounded the corner Malice stopped and looked at Lucien.

"What's up?"

Lucien exhaled, ran his hand over the back of his neck, and looked out the back window. "I've talked to Kink, so me telling you this doesn't go against his privacy, and besides, you need to know why he was all fucked-up back at the meeting. He doesn't really care who knows, but he hasn't said anything to the other members yet, and neither have I."

"Okay, what's going on?" Malice knitted his brows and crossed his arms over his chest. "You talking about that attitude shit that happened between us back there?"

Lucien nodded. "Yeah." He shook his head, stopping Malice from responding. "Just hear me out."

Malice gritted his teeth and nodded.

"Kink is in a bad place right now."

"We all are, aren't we?" Malice leaned against the wall and sighed. Fuck, he was tired of all the fucking drama that seemed to surround them on a daily basis.

"Yeah, and I'm not downplaying anyone else's shit. But then my VP and enforcer are going at each other's throat for stupid fucking shit, and I can't have that." Lucien shook his head, and a dark mask covered his face. "Not cool, and I'm not about to put up with that shit."

"I know, and I'm sorry about that, but no fucking way anyone will talk to me, or about Adrianna that way." Malice felt this twisted confusion inside of him, one that made no sense, but that he didn't want to ignore or end. He stared at Lucien, and the dark mask that had covered his President's face was now gone, and there was almost an understanding on his expression.

"And I wouldn't have put up with that shit either if I had an old lady." Lucien exhaled. "Listen, I don't have a woman, probably never will to be honest, so I can't see having this possessive need to protect them like that. None of the guys seem to want to settle down either, but I've been with the MC a long fucking time, have seen the older members take on old ladies and love them like the world was ending." Lucien leaned against the wall, too. "I mean my dad was the last person I would have thought would settle down."

Malice smiled and nodded. "Yeah, he was one tough asshole."

Lucien started laughing, and despite the tough exterior he always wore, Malice saw the slight pain cover his face. It was after Brandon "Ranger" Silver had passed away of a heart attack last year that Lucien had gotten in contact with other Nomads and started this charter up with the blessing from The Brothers of Menace. Lucien may have never really said why he had started this charter, but in the end it didn't matter. It could have been a lot of different reasons: tired of always being alone, wanting that family circle back again, or just needing to have a purpose with his own MC. Whatever the reason was, they were here now, and things in that department were looking good.

"Tilly and your mom are doing well?" Malice asked about Lucien's half-sister and his mom, who lived in Thornton.

He shrugged. "As good as can be I assume. Haven't seen them really since we set up shop in River Run, but I know Tilly is busy with finishing up her degree, and my mom is doing fine. She and Marshall are adding an addition to the house so his grandkids can have a place to stay when they visit."

Malice didn't go into any more detail about Lucien's mother's husband. She may have been an old lady to Ranger at one time, but the MC life wasn't for everyone.

"Anyway, back to why I wanted to talk to you."

Malice didn't miss the fact Lucien changed the subject. "Sarah is planning on moving to California with that dead-beat boyfriend she has, and taking Kink's kid with her."

"Shit." Just the thought of some asshole trying to take his kid, would have had Malice on a murderous rampage. He might have had issues at first with Stinger, Molly's now old man, but things had settled down, and he respected the Grizzly MC member. But that wasn't to say that if Stinger tried to stop him from seeing Dakota, or God forbid take his kid away… Malice tightened his arms across his chest and forced himself to push those thoughts out of his head. They weren't real, and he wasn't going to let them make him even more pissed. "I can see why he is on edge."

Lucien grunted. "Yeah, seems like all this shit is going down in a short amount of time, but maybe that means we are getting all the drama out early."

Yeah, Malice really doubted that. "Listen, I am not in the best of moods either, but my issues are nothing compared to what Kink is going through. I should have kept my cool, but—"

"It's done, brother," Lucien said in a solid, straightforward tone. They stared at each other for a moment, and then Lucien grinned. "But an old lady, huh?"

Malice shook his head. "Never thought I'd want another woman, hell not even after a few days, but I feel something for that girl. Pretty fucking crazy, huh?"

Lucian shook his head. "Nah. Look at the life we lead. We are surrounded by danger constantly, and it isn't like doing all that immoral shit doesn't weigh heavily on us." He shrugged. "We are a different breed of male, Malice. We fight with our hearts, ride with pleasure because it is in our blood, and fuck with abandon." There was no humor in Lucien's words, because what he said was truer than most things. Lucien had this look on his face.

"What?"

He shrugged. "Nothing." Lucien ran his hand over the back of his neck. "Well, that isn't true. I've just never seen you this … enamored, not even when you were with Molly."

"Enamored?" Malice grinned. "I don't think I've ever heard you use a word that big."

Lucien flipped him off, but he cracked a smile. "Fuck you. Anyway, that was what I wanted to tell you. Give him space, let him work out his shit, and I know he'll do the same with you." Lucien took a step forward and placed a hand on his shoulder, and then turned and went back to the main room.

Malice stood there for a few minutes replaying what Lucien said in his head. Yeah, he had known Adrianna was something different and special when he first looked into her face. It wasn't just about wanting to protect her, or wanting to fuck her in the worst kind of way like he was some kind of dirty bastard. He liked being around her, liked the things she made him feel even though she had no clue the effect she had on him.

"Fuck." He pushed off the wall and made his way to one of the empty bedrooms. Maybe his head would be in the game with a few hours of sleep under his belt? If not, well, then he was going to have to deal with what he felt for Adrianna, and see where in the hell it took him.

## Chapter Eleven

Malice sat on the opposite side of Adrianna, and watched as she smiled and thanked everyone who offered her a dish of food. Tatum, a woman who had once started out as a club whore but was now an employee of the MC, now cooked, cleaned, and did their laundry. She was older, and was now more of a den mother to everyone that hung around the club. But Tatum took care of them even though they lived like slobs and did a bunch of shit that would make their mothers slap their faces. He leaned back in his seat, already having had his fill of the meal, and couldn't help but just watch Adrianna. She looked relaxed and comfortable, and he was glad because the last thing he wanted was for her to feel out of place amongst a bunch of roughened bikers. He glanced at Kink, and from the scrapes and bruises it was clear he had come from a fight. But if that's how he eased the pain he felt, then it wasn't anyone else's business. He turned his focus back to Adrianna, and saw that she was speaking to Tatum.

"You've been here long?" Adrianna asked the other woman.

She shrugged. "This clubhouse has only been up and running for the last few months, but I've known all these guys for years. I used to hang around another charter until I hooked up with them."

Tatum grabbed her glass of wine. For forty-eight she looked good for her age.

The sound around them intensified as laughter rang out, jokes were told, and the whole atmosphere of the clubhouse went from tense and heavy to light and joyous. It was these times that Malice lived for. He saw that Adrianna was fully immersed in a story that Tatum was telling her, and he couldn't help but watch her. He got hard just watching her sit there, and what a creepy as hell thing to do. A fucking mundane act made his damn cock like steel. And her fucking mouth… He ran a hand over his jaw and stared at those lush, red lips. He hadn't been able to *not* think about it since their kiss.

Like some kind of sick fuck that couldn't get enough of her, he watched as she set her fork down and kept talking to Tatum. But everything else narrowed, and he had tunnel vision as he followed the length of her arm, and moved his gaze over the creamy swatch of skin that he could see above the collar of her shirt. Damn, her collarbones had his tongue actually swelling with the need to run it across those delicate bones. He had always thought that part of the female body was attractive, but on Adrianna it was tenfold. Her breasts pressed snugly against the top Tatum had given her, and he forced himself to pull his gaze away from her and stop being a bastard. But when he looked at her face it was to see her staring at him. He should have felt ashamed for checking her out, but he knew she wanted him just as badly as he wanted her. That was clear when they kissed.

She turned and stared at him then, as if she had felt his gaze on her. They stared at each other for several long seconds. Tuck sat beside him, and although Malice heard the other man speaking to him, he was honestly lost in his own fucked-up world. God, what he wouldn't give to have Adrianna right now, but he wouldn't be rough and hard with her like he was accustomed to with other women. He'd be gentle, and touch her so she knew that this wasn't just about sticking his dick in her and getting off. He wanted her to be right there with him, to feel everything he did to her and plead for more. Malice wanted her breath to coast along his sweat-soaked skin, and he wanted her nails to be deep in his body as she held on while he slowly pushed inside of her sweet body and pulled out with just as much anguished detail. His breathing started to increase as those images played through his mind, but to him it was just him and Adrianna at this table. Everything else faded in the background. She still watched him, and he noticed the subtle changes in her to alert him to the fact she was growing aroused, too. If he felt this much lust pounding through his veins no doubt she could see the physical signs of it, too.

"Malice."

His name being said beside him more firmly had Malice snapping out of the haze and turning to look at Tuck. The other man was leaning back in his chair, this cocky smirk on his face.

He leaned forward, and in a low voice that only Malice could hear said, "Get your shit together, man. You look like you are about to jump across this table and mount Adrianna in front of everyone."

Malice glowered at Tuck, but didn't look at Adrianna again. He did need to get himself under control, but the truth was he felt like he was a teenager all over again that had just gotten his dick wet and didn't know how to keep cool. He nodded once, and when Tuck was leaning back in his chair again he grabbed his napkin, wiped his face, and excused himself. He'd go to the bathroom and jerk off like an asshole, and try to ease this need for her enough that he could actually be a foot from her and not feel like his dick would tear right through his jeans. He still hadn't talked to her yet about him wanting her as his old lady, and honestly he didn't know how she would react. Yeah, she might want him, but sexual need was a hell of a lot different from being his old lady. Maybe she just saw him as this knight in shining white armor that had saved her? Maybe she wanted him because of a psychological thing? Like she connected with him because he saved her? He scrubbed a hand over his face and moved down the hallway. He didn't know shit about that kind of stuff, but what he did know was that he wouldn't know for sure what she wanted with him unless he talked to her. The sooner he did it the better he could put his mind and his hard-on at ease.

****

"This is bullshit, Sarah." Kink paced right outside of the barn, and inhaled angrily from his cigarette.

"It's not, Kink. I have found someone that makes me happy, and if that means I have to go with him to California to stay happy then I am."

He inhaled again, and exhaled just as harshly. "I don't care if you are happy or not, or if you fucking move, but taking my kid all way to another fucking state because you have been dating a guy for a total of three damn months, is not going to fucking fly." Kink was beyond pissed. He thought calling her and talking about this—again—would help things. He had been dead fucking wrong. He should have just gone over there again and demanded this bullshit be put to rest.

"You don't have a choice in this. I have custody, and she is a minor—"

"If I have to take you to court to make sure you don't run off with her I will."

She sighed, and that annoyed sound grated on his nerves. "I don't want a custody battle, and I don't want to make this a war, Kink."

"Then if you don't want a war don't take my kid."

He could hear her pencil dick motherfucking boyfriend telling her to hang up on him because she didn't need to hear his bullshit. "You tell that asshole to get on the phone if he wants to start spouting off things." He curled his hand into a fist and gritted his teeth. "I can show him exactly how much of an asshole I really am."

"Stop being so damn dramatic. I can see where Callie gets her fucking drama from." She sighed again. There was some static from her covering the phone so she could talk to the douche bag boyfriend, and then she stated talking once more. "Callie could use a change of scenery anyway. Her attitude has gotten to the point that I can hardly handle it, and I think her boyfriend is in a gang."

That had him stopping. "She has a boyfriend?" *Oh hell no.* He snubbed his cigarette out on the bottom of his boot and moved toward the side of the barn. The shouts were loud and energized from guys watching others beat the shit out of each other.

"He's new, and the first one she's brought around. But her attitude is horrible, and ever since telling her about California she has gotten worse."

"Yeah, no fucking shit. You're taking her away months before she graduates because you're a selfish bitch."

"Hey, fuck you, Kink. Sleeping with you was a mistake, and letting it carry on for as long as it did was a mistake, too."

His heart beat faster as his anger exploded inside of him. "The only good thing about being with you for those couple of weeks is Callie. Other than that it was a big damn mistake for me, too." He couldn't even call what they had shared a relationship. A few weeks of sex—and that one time he had fucked her without a condom because he had been drunk—had been a damn nightmare. But then she had gotten pregnant, and when Callie was born something changed inside of him. He was a dad to a little girl that looked up to him. He might not be the best role model, and might belong to an outlaw MC, but he was there for her, and would die if it meant she could live. She was the one ray of light in his otherwise clusterfuck life.

"If you want to drag your daughter through a court hearing, make her traumatized that her lowlife biker father wants to make a damn scene over this, then go ahead and make a fucking scene, Kink. Do whatever you have to do, but in the end who do you think the courts will side with?" He didn't say anything, but she started speaking again before he could spout off a string of profanities. "You belong to a motorcycle club that has a reputation of being involved in illegal and dangerous activity. I've told you that I was talking to my lawyer, and I meant it, Kink. She is drafting documents up for the judge about moving out of state with Callie."

"You are one cold hearted bitch."

"I will do what I have to do to ensure that my happiness isn't fucked up by you. I mean, you fucked up my life as it is by getting me knocked up and being an absentee father."

He gritted his teeth again, willing himself not to say what was really on his mind because it would only make the situation worse. "I'm only going to tell you this once, Sarah."

"Say whatever you want, Kink. It doesn't matter either way."

"You will not take my kid from me." He disconnected the call and nearly crushed the cell in his hand. He would go to drastic measures if it meant keeping his kid close. He turned and slammed his fist into the side of the barn. He loved the pain, but it didn't make him feel any better.

The crowd went wild right on the other side of the wall he leaned against, and he pushed away from the barn and walked around the building. He was enraged, and needed a good fucking fight to get it out of him. He pushed the people out of his way once inside, and lucky for him the fight commencing was just ending. Tilting his head toward a few of The Grizzly MC members, and some Brothers prospects, he walked up to them. Rock was getting himself pumped up to take the center by jumping on the balls of his feet, cracking his knuckles, and rolling his head around on his neck.

"I need to be next." Kink ground the words out and glanced at Rock. The other biker looked like he might argue, but when he saw the clear anger on Kink's face he nodded and held his hands up.

"All yours, brother."

Kink took his cut and shirt off and held it out to Pierce. He moved forward just as the other brothers dragged their sorry asses out of the center of the bar. He faced off with the fighter that stepped forward. *Come on, motherfucker, let's do this.*

The other guy wasted no time and charged forward. Kink slammed his fist into the other fighter's face, and felt the surge of adrenaline flood his body from the impact. It felt good to deliver violence, felt fucking fantastic to see the blood pour out of the other man's nose because he had just broken it. He slammed his fist into the other guy's face again and again until blood covered his knuckles, splattered across his bare chest, and made him feel even more alive. His rage kept building, kept taking control until there was no sane and logical part of him left.

He hit the man again and loved that his eyes rolled back and he fell to the ground. He was still so juiced up, still needed to kick another motherfucker's ass because he wasn't nearly done yet. He'd try to talk to Sarah again, reasoning with her that Callie should just stay with him until she graduated, and then she could decide where she wanted to start her life. Normally he just took what he wanted. Callie was *his* kid, and no way in hell he'd let his daughter leave. He turned in a circle and bounced on the balls of his feet. Starring at all the guys lined up to fight, he grinned, hoping they took note that he loved the blood on him. Some looked apprehensive, others tried to look unaffected, but it made no difference because he'd take as many of them out that had the balls to come into the center and brawl with him. He lived for this shit, volunteered to fight every damn night if it meant he could kick someone's ass. He had done this for money back in the day, back before he committed himself to the MC. These fights were straight-out street rules, and that was exactly how Kink liked it.

"What motherfucker is ready to hit the floor next?"

The crowd went wild, and money was raised high as the volume increased tenfold. The guy that stepped forward looked far too little to be fighting dirty at the barn, but what the fuck ever. The end result would always be the same. He didn't prance around what was happening, just held his fists up, grinned at the prick, and threw a left hook, and then a right undercut. The other guy fell back on his ass without even being given the opportunity to throw a punch.

"Get up, asshole." Sweat dripped down Kink's temples, and he tasted the metallic, tangy flavor of blood in his mouth from the last guy that had managed to hit him. The other guy finally pulled his sorry ass off the ground, and turned his head to spit out a mouthful of blood. The crowd went wild once again, and he had to give the scrawny fuck some credit for having balls. More sweat dripped off his bare chest and fell to the rust stained colored ground. The other guy suddenly charged forward. He swung left, and then right, but Kink easily dodged the attempt. This barn might mainly be used for shifter fights, but Kink was about to show these fuckers that humans were some bad motherfuckers, too. The other fighter caught him in the jaw, and Kink stumbled back. His lip split, and blood dripped down his chin. So this little shit had some bite in him. Good, because Kink didn't like things to be easy.

Kink ran the back of his hand over his mouth, and noticed the blood smeared across it. "I hope you enjoyed that hit, because it is the only one you're going to get." He charged forward, saw the fighter's eyes widen before he slammed his fist into the side of his head. The guy stumbled backward, and Kink could have easily kept going, but he didn't want to kill the guy. The guy lay passed out on the floor, and a bloody mess. Spectators roared out for more, exchanged money, and then the next guy stepped into the proverbial ring. Yeah, Kink was going to go all fucking night until he couldn't stand straight, couldn't think, and all of the anger had left him—well, until he saw that fucking bitch Sarah again.

## Chapter Twelve

Adrianna had nothing to her name, not anymore at least. No money, no bag with personal possessions. Nothing. The only thing she had was the fresh clothes on her back that Tatum had given her this morning. But now, as she stared around at this gorgeous two-story cabin out in the middle of the woods, she felt the generosity that was shown to her clog her throat and have tears forming in her eyes. But to be fair she had been on the verge of tears since Malice had told her that this would be her new home for the time being, and that she could make some money by helping with the cooking, cleaning, and anything else that needed to be done around the place. And even though at first he tried to tell her to just rest, get her bearings, and they would worry about keeping her busy with the cabin stuff another time, she wasn't having any of that. She wanted to be able to contribute, and if that meant doing housework then she was more than happy to do it.

She thought about Malice. He had been kind of standoffish around her since he left the dinner table last evening. She hadn't seen him again last night, but that was probably for the best. The way he had looked at her across the table, like some kind of lion about to pounce on her, had been a look no man had ever given her. No man except Malice. Even now she still felt her lips tingle from their kiss, and still felt her clit throb from unrestrained and unfulfilled desire. It had only been a few days since she had left Fairview, and although outside she was healing, she needed to work on healing herself on the inside.

"What do you think?" Malice stood beside her and she glanced over at him. The light came through the window, shadowing the front half of him and almost giving him this sinister, highly seductive appearance. He turned and looked at her when she did respond. "Adrianna?"

Blinking and then smiling, she turned back to the great room. Right now they stood in the foyer of the cabin Malice had told her women who were rehabilitating stayed in. They hadn't really spoken much, and she really didn't know why the club would be in the business of having some kind of half-way house in the middle of nowhere. But of course she wasn't a fool. She assumed enough that this had something to do with illegal affairs, ones that probably lined their pockets. The why of it was what she didn't exactly know.

"It's beautiful." She looked around the house, saw several women cleaning up, others reading in little nooks, or just sitting on the couch and talking with each other. She turned back to Malice. "What exactly is this place?" When he didn't answer right away she went on. "I mean I know you said it was where these women could heal, but I don't understand what that means." She had lowered her voice so only he could hear.

He tipped his chin toward the stairs, and she followed him. They climbed the stairs, and she didn't miss how some of the women glanced her way, and then looked at Malice. Once they reached the top of the stairs he moved down the hallway and stopped on the last door on the right. The room they entered was gorgeous in the natural, bare sense. A full bed was against the wall, a matching pine dresser across from that, and a large window that showed the front part of the property. She walked over to the window, saw the two bikers she had noticed when they first pulled up leaning against the smaller cabin beside this house, and then heard the door shut behind her. She turned and saw Malice standing right in front of it.

"I probably should have told you all of this before now," he shrugged, "but now is as good a time as any, I suppose. " He gestured toward the bed, and she moved toward it and sat down. For a few seconds he didn't say anything, but then he went over to the closet and pulled the door open. Inside she could see clothes hanging even though he hadn't turned on the light. "When we had this place fixed up and the rooms made we got some clothes for the women that would be staying here. I don't know if any of them will fit you. Most of the girls have already had their pick, so basically this is the leftover stuff, but if nothing fits I'll take you to get some things."

"Thank you, but I'm sure it will be fine. I'll make it work."

He looked at her over his shoulder. "I told you what this place was, that it was to make sure the women here could heal and get back on their feet."

She nodded, feeling her nerves go on alert because what he had to say couldn't be good, right?

He turned fully around, stared out the window from across the room for several seconds, and then took a few steps toward her. "The MC makes most of its living selling women, Adrianna."

For a second she just blinked, and then blinked some more. Trying to comprehend what he had just said wasn't hard. She had heard him clearly, but the thought of selling women was so abhorrent to her, and reminded her of the grimy life she had fled, that everything inside of her instinctually told her to leave right now.

"We don't keep these women here against their will, Adrianna."

That comforted her a little, even though she had hoped, and known deep down, that that hadn't been the case. She may not have been sold, but she had watched her mother sell her body for extra money, watched the men come in and out of their hovel of a home, and didn't want to be a part of that anymore. She was moving away from that.

"The club does have a house out past Steel Corner. We use the town as a transport line to get there so we stay off the highways."

There was clearly this awkwardness coming from him, and it was a little strange seeing him uncomfortable. Since she had met him he had always seemed so in control of everything, including himself.

"The women that work for us are there because they want to be. We treat them well, they are paid and protected, and if at any time they ever want to leave they are free to go."

Adrianna had every reason to believe him. He had done nothing but help her from the moment they met. Besides, the women that had been reading, laughing and talking, and cleaning certainly hadn't looked like they were here held against their will. They also didn't look beaten as Malice had said happened to them, but just because she couldn't see any marks didn't mean they hadn't suffered. She knew that reality just as well as anyone. It didn't take a genius to put two-and-two together. "Those women were beaten by their former pimps?"

Malice sighed, nodded, and moved to sit on the bed beside her. "Yeah, but they won't ever be hurt again." He looked over at her, and she felt how true his words were. She felt them as deeply as she had felt that truth when he had told her that about Phillip. "So, the club fixed this place up so they would have somewhere safe to stay."

"What about when they want to go?"

"Then the door is always open. If they want to stay and work doing domestic things, we find them work.

If they want to go back to what they were doing before—
" He paused for a second before continuing. "Then we
can help them out in that regards, too."

She looked away from him for a second,
processing his words. "I can't imagine wanting to go
back to prostituting myself after being beaten." But as
soon as the words left her she squeezed her eyes shut. She
may not have sold her body, but she had stayed with
Phillip far too long, even after he had hurt her the first
time. Of course she knew why someone would want to go
back to what they felt comfortable doing, and what had
been their life for probably a long time. When she looked
back at Malice she saw this worried expression on his
face, and she smiled, letting him know without words that
she wasn't about to flip. "Does your club have a doctor
that comes and checks on them?"

Malice shook his head, but looked away for her.
"No, well, we have a doctor that works with the club on
the down low, but Molly is a nurse and comes by every
week to spend some time with them and see if they are
okay."

Adrianna wouldn't have thought anything of a
nurse coming here. It made sense even to have a medical
professional on their payroll, but Malice acted strangely
when he said her name, and Adrianna knew right away
there was obviously some kind of history between them.

He turned his attention back to her. "My ex,
Molly, she moved to Steel Corner with our three year old
son after she became the old lady to a club The Brothers
are associates with."

Son and ex-old lady.

Not that she was surprised he had a child, or
uncomfortable with that idea. The little conversation they
had here and there, and even during the van ride from
Fairview to River Run had consisted of them telling each

other little facts about each other. But of course she had left out the less favorable things, and clearly he had left out the major stuff as well. He was older than she was by almost two decades, so of course he would have had a family. "Do you get to see your son often?" The way his expression eased and the worry lines around his eyes smoothed had his heart warming. He loved his son greatly, and that kind of love was strong enough that it reached out to whoever was close by and wrapped them in an embrace.

He smiled, and she couldn't help but reciprocate the act. "When Molly lived in Brighton I only saw him every other weekend and occasionally on the weekdays. It was hard getting down there since it's five hours away." He shrugged. "But she's just in Steel Corner now."

"That's pretty close?" Adrianna liked sitting here just talking with him. There was still that desire inside of her, but this comfortableness that surrounded them and the easygoing nature that came from Malice was nice.

"Just the next town over."

"I bet he's really excited that he gets to see his dad more now."

Malice grinned even wider, and although she felt many emotions, happiness and relief, as well as arousal and content, she also felt a twinge of sadness.

"Hey."

She hadn't realized she had looked down until she felt Malice's finger on her chin. He lifted her head and turned it so she was looking at him again.

"What's the matter? Did I say something to make you upset?"

A humorless chuckle left her, and he knitted his brows in confusion. She shook her head and closed her eyes for a few seconds before opening them. "I'm not laughing at you. It's just if I would have seen you on the street I would have thought you were this rough and tough biker, and run the other way." She smiled, but it was shaky as her emotion still ran high through her.

"I am a rough and tough biker." He was looking at her mouth, but even though his words were low they held truth.

"Yes, I know, but you also have this other side."

He slowly lifted his gaze back to her face.

"You're very sweet and gentle, and that kind of goes against the leather wearing, tattoo covered skin thing going on." When she chuckled this time it held more amusement. But he didn't laugh or crack a smile, and just continued to stare at her. The need to be open with the man that had saved her life ran hard through her, and she actually found herself opening her mouth and speaking about her brother for the first time to anyone since he had passed away. "I don't have any children, but I had a younger brother." Malice didn't say anything, but she was thankful for that because she might not have had the strength to continuing if he tried to delve into this himself. "Our life was what one could call trashy." Shaking her head and smiling this very forced one, she continued. "Fairview is a nice town, but every place as its downfall, and where we lived was that place. Drugs, sex, violence, all of that and more were a daily occurrence." His hand laced with hers, and Adrianna smiled at that feeling and sight. It felt nice and calming, and she was glad she was telling him this. Maybe it really didn't matter if he knew this dark side of her life, but she felt better getting it out. "Long story short Miles got involved in drugs, and one night had too much." The tears she had kept inside for years finally broke free, and she felt ridiculous.

"Hey. Shhh." Malice had his arms around her and pulled her close so her body was pressed to his in a matter of seconds. Here he was being all sweet again despite the almost scary exterior he emitted. But that went to show that the outside appearance wasn't what someone should focus on.

Everything rushed through her as her emotions were open and vulnerable.

"I'm sorry, baby."

She should have been stunned at the endearment he had just called her, but she tightened her arms around him. He smelled good, like spicy, dark cologne, and something familiar that she couldn't quite place.

"Everything will be okay now." He rubbed her back in slow sweeps of his hand, and she forced herself to pull away and look into his face.

"I don't have money, Malice, and I already feel so indebted to you." The worry about paying him and his club back for everything they had and were doing for her was this heavy weight on her shoulders.

"That isn't something to worry about right now, baby." He brushed his thumb under her eye and collected her tear. "But when you feel like you're ready, you have a job here."

"Here?"

Cupping her face with each hand he stared into her eyes with his gray gaze. "The club already approves it, but if you want to work, since you've mentioned that already, you could work *here*, be employed by the club to help take care of the women and the house."

"But what about when they are healed and ready to move on? What happens to the cabin then?"

He shook his head. "Then that is great when they are healed and gone, but this house is still going to be used as *their* home. The women that weren't hurt—the ones that work for the club—still need a stable place to call home. This is that place. There are always Brothers making sure everyone is safe." He stroked his thumbs across her cheeks. "And knowing you're here, safe from all the fucking ugliness of the world, will help me sleep better at night."

His dark hair was longer, and she moved her hands up and brushed the tips of the strands with her fingers. "I don't even know what to say." Honestly, she hadn't thought anything like this would happen so easily for her. Up until this point she hadn't had it easy, but ever since meeting Malice things had just kind of fallen into place.

"Money is not something you need to worry about right now, and paying me or the club back isn't something you need to worry about ever. All I want you to focus on is getting better, but if you really want to press it, you can get a wage to help around here. I know it would help the girls that are a little more unstable than the rest. But I meant what I said that I want you to heal and not worry about anything." He stared at her, and then gave her this crooked smile that made her heart race. "However long that takes is up to you, and no one will rush you on that. You're strong, Adrianna, and the women here need that strength to help find their own."

"I'm a far cry from being strong, Malice. In fact, I can't count the number of times I've been called a doormat." This very frightening and hard look crossed his face, and she swallowed.

"You don't every think about yourself like that." His voice was deep and angry. "If you were so weak you wouldn't have left, and you wouldn't have been strong enough to realize that you deserved so much more."

Her heart felt like it was going to burst right through her chest. "You act like you care." She didn't mean it in a condescending or ungrateful way. She meant it in the context that she was surprised someone like him—a stranger that had opened up his heart to her—actually gave a shit what happened to her.

"I do care, Adrianna." He lowered his gaze to her mouth again. "I care a fucking lot, in fact." He leaned in an inch so there was hardly any space separating their mouths. "You deserve a hell of a lot better than the likes of me, but I'm a selfish bastard and I want you for my own."

"Malice—"

"And I won't let you go, Adrianna. I can't." He pressed his mouth to hers right after the last word left his lips.

## Chapter Thirteen

The kiss was so very possessive, and it was like Malice was placing this brand of ownership on her. He swept his tongue along her upper lip. "I wanted to do that since the last time I had you in my arms."

Adrianna couldn't even control her breathing let alone tell him that she had been thinking about their kiss since it had happened, too. He moved his hand around her shoulder and pressed his open palm to the small of her back. Even through her clothing she could feel his body heat, sensed how big his hand really was, and got lost in the smooth and easy way he kissed her. Would he care that she wasn't skinny like the women she saw working at the club? Adrianna always was on the thicker side, and Phillip had always made sure she knew how fat he thought she was. Would Malice be disgusted that she had curves she wasn't always proud of, or that she was disgusted with her body sometimes? She could sense that he was keeping himself back in the way he kept clenching and unclenching his other hand on her shoulder, and by the pressure of his fingers that were at the base of her spine. She liked this soft side of him, but she'd be lying if she didn't admit that she liked when he had taken action and control in the van—like he was doing right now as he applied more pressure and growled low in his throat. Adrianna wanted to be kissed with abandon, like he would never be able to get enough of her, because she sure as hell wouldn't be able to get enough of him.

"I want you so fucking badly, Adrianna." He stood suddenly, pulled her so her chest was flush with his, and ground his erection into her belly. A small whimper let her at the feel of his shaft so hard because he wanted her that badly.

The words for him to take her right here and now were on the tip of her tongue, but before she could say anything he had his tongue deep inside of her mouth and swallowed them up. For several long, drugging seconds he kissed her thoroughly, and the stroking and thrusting he did with his tongue and hip were reminiscent of what she wanted him to do with another part of his body between her thighs. She had her hands on his biceps, loved that they were so strong, so rock hard with muscle that she couldn't even hold onto a portion of them they were so big. He moved them so she was forced to walk backwards, and when she felt the wall greet her, a soft sound escaped her. Malice broke the kiss, trailed his mouth down her jaw and over her neck, and proceeded to suck and bite at her throat.

"Oh, God." She gasped out as her pussy became soaked from her need to have him.

"I want to taste you." He moved his hand over her breasts, curled his fingers around the mound until she groaned out, and then continued to trail it down her belly. He stopped when he was right above her pussy, and her inner muscles clenched at the knowledge he was so close to what she wanted him to touch the most.

"I want you to taste me, Malice." She hadn't meant to say that out loud, but as soon as the words left her he groaned and placed his open palm right between her legs. The pants she wore were nothing but thin, stretchy cotton, and she could feel the heat from his body sear right to the center of hers.

"Say it again." He murmured against her neck, and went back to running his tongue up and down the length of her throat and nipping her flesh along the way. "Tell me you want my mouth on your pussy, how you want me pulling your lips apart and sucking your clit into my mouth."

Adrianna couldn't hold her head up any longer and let it fall back against the wall. Closing her eyes and not able to stop the moan that left her, she opened her mouth to obey him. God, she wanted to say just that, but her clit started throbbing from the increased blood flow, and her nipples ached painfully as they hardened even further. "I…" She swallowed when he applied even more pressure to her pussy and pressed the base of his palm right against her clit. "Oh." The one word came from her on an exhale.

"That's all right, baby." He kissed his way down her throat, over her collarbone, and then dragged his tongue over the raised bone. "I know you want it, can feel how wet you are through your pants, and don't blame you for not being able to speak." His breath was hot, humid, and when he spoke it was more akin to panting. "I can barely speak myself." He didn't move for a moment and just breathed in and out. "I love your body, love your curves and that you're built like a woman." He groaned and squeezed his hands on her flesh. "I love that you are built to take me into your body and not break."

God, he was saying all the right things to make her so very plaint to him. He took her hand that was on his bicep, and moved it between their bodies and right over his dick. She swore the damn thing jumped beneath her palm, and a fresh gush of moisture left her.

"You feel how hard you make me?" He emphasized his point by pressing himself more firmly against her hand. "I don't think I've ever been this hard in my life."

The way he spoke to her was so erotic that Adrianna actually found herself cupping him through his jeans and moaning at the large size she was greeted with. But to her disappointment he continued moving down her body, which had her hand falling back to her side, and stopped when he was on his haunches right in front of her

"Look at me, Adrianna." He spoke with this harsh, guttural tone, and Adrianna couldn't help but obey.

She opened her eyes and looked down, and when she watched him take the edge of her pants between his fingers and started to pull them down, the air got trapped in her lungs. "This is so fast."

He stopped instantly, but still held her pants and held his gaze with his own. "If you want me to stop I will, baby. You are controlling this situation, and you hold all the power."

Hearing a man as strong as Malice say she was in control had a wave of strength moving through her. It was very empowering to know that she had this large and dangerous man in the palm of her hands. This was not like any situation she had ever experienced, and the things she felt were completely foreign to her. But what she knew without a doubt was that she wasn't going to stop this. Placing both of her hands over his, she started to push her pants down. Malice flared his nostrils, and then looked down when the material fell past her knees and her panties were the only thing covering her from him. The only thing she could hear was their combined rapid breathing, and then Malice was pulling her panties down and the chilled air was touching her exposed flesh.

"Oh, *Christ*, baby."

She looked down at him after he groaned out those three words. He stared at her pussy, and then slowly moved his hands toward her, kept one right by the junction of where her leg met her body, and then moved the other to the back of her thigh and down behind her knee. He lifted her leg, removed her foot from her pants and panties, and then placed her leg over his shoulder. He didn't give her much time to contemplate what was happening, because in a matter of seconds he had a hold of her ass, and was dragging his tongue through her now parted folds. He breathed out on a growl that vibrated every part of her. To have him pay so much attention to pleasuring her had euphoria slamming into her with enough force that if he wasn't holding on to her she would have fallen to the ground.

"Hold on to me, baby," he said against the small, engorged nub. He licked her clit over and over again, sucked it into his mouth until she was about to come, and then backed off. Adrianna had her hands in his hair, tugged at the strands so they became tangled in her fingers, and gasped in pleasure. She had to be hurting him by the way she was forcefully pulling at his hair, and when she went to let go he made this almost angry noise in the back of his throat.

"No, keep your hands there. I like the fact you're hurting me because you can't control yourself from the way I make you feel." He licked her again, and again, and God once more. When he flattened his tongue and dragged it from the opening of her pussy all the way to her clit, and then repeated the action, her body coiled tight. She was going to come in a matter of seconds if he kept that up, but as if she said those words to him he slowed his ministrations, and lessened the pressure. "You want to come, don't you, Adrianna?"

He was teasing her, torturing her, and she wasn't below begging him to let her get off. "*Yes.*" It was pleasure and pain, ecstasy and agony all rolled into one, and Adrianna knew that she'd scream loud enough that the whole house would be able to hear her once she finally climaxed. Using the hand that had been supporting her ass, he moved it around and right to the opening of her body, and then he was pushing a thick finger into her pussy.

"So fucking tight and hot." He sucked on her clit and pumped that finger in and out of her. "And so damn soaked for me." He slowly added another digit until she felt so very full. It might only be two fingers he had lodged into of her body, but Malice was a big man, and his hands and fingers were no different. He started pumping into her and retreating, sucking on the bud at the top of her mound and humming against it.

"Oh God. Malice." She gasped out his name just as the first wave of pleasure slammed into her.

"That's it, fucking come all over my face."

She opened her mouth as stars danced in front of her vision, ready to cry out because she couldn't help herself, but before she could make a sound Malice had his hand on her mouth. He muffled the sound of her crying out, but he never stopped eating her out.

"*Christ*." He grunted. "You're getting wetter."

"Oh." That word was muffled against his palm, and as the ecstasy rose to a fever pitch she found herself pressing her pussy further and harder into his face. Before the pleasure receded he was standing, removing his hand from her mouth, and pressing his lips to hers. She could taste herself on him, that salty muskiness of her arousal that coated his mouth and tongue. They groaned at the same time, and Adrianna still had a hold on his hair. She wasn't gentle, and wanted to show him that she had enjoyed and wanted more of what he had just given her.

"I will never get enough of that, baby." He opened his mouth wider, used his hand on her chin to tilt her head to the side, and plunged his tongue deep into her mouth. For long, drugging seconds that was all they did, and it was only when she heard the sound of women right on the other side of the door did she pull away. The women were laughing, talking about things that were too muffled to hear through the door, but it was all that

Adrianna needed for reality to set in. He pulled back so he could look in her face. "I'm not nearly done with you yet. Not by a fucking long shot."

Her mouth felt swollen and warm, and she knew that her lips had to be red. "I don't want you to be done with me." The attraction she had felt for him had been instant, but she was willing to take a risk and see where this went with them. She wanted it really badly, in fact.

He took a step back, ran his thumb over the corner of her mouth, and then leaned in and kissed her softly once more. "I'm going to go so you can get settled in, but I have something for you." He reached into his leather vest and produced a cell phone and a scrap piece of paper. "I want you to call me if you need anything." He held the phone up. "I mean it, Adrianna. You call me, and I'll make sure you get it."

"What if I want you?" Damn, she could have slapped a hand over her mouth for saying that. The smirk that moved across his face couldn't be called anything but deadly, but it was of the erotic variety, and it had a tingle moving through her pussy. She might have just had an orgasm, but it felt like she hadn't even scratched the surface.

He had his chest pressed to hers instantly, his mouth by her ear, and his hand wrapped loosely around the nape of her neck. "You call me, baby." His warm breath moved along the shell of her ear. "You call, and I am here in ten minutes." He pulled back slightly, not enough that she could see his face. With his cheek pressed to her, the feel of his trimmed beard scraped her sensitive skin, but she loved it, because it reminded her that she was actually here with him. "I'd be lying through my teeth if I told you I didn't want you to call me all the time. Just hearing your voice makes me hard, but it also makes my heart beat fast." He grabbed her hand and put it right over his chest. "Say something," he whispered.

For a second she just breathed, but then licked her lips and said, "I don't want you to go." And then she actually felt his heart start to beat faster, and felt his still erect dick against her belly.

"I know, but I'm only a phone call away. I have some club stuff to deal with, but I will be back tomorrow. I'll call you in the morning and check in on you, but if you need me in the meantime call me." He took a step back to her disappointment.

"Okay." They stared at each other for a moment, and then he smiled, a genuine one that had her growing pliant.

"I'll see you later, baby." He turned and left, shutting the door behind him and leaving Adrianna with her pants and panties pooled around one leg, and her lust renewed once more. Malice was bad news, but only in the best kind of way.

## Chapter Fourteen

Malice helped Tuck and Rock load the last of the supplies that would be taken to the whorehouse that they had past Steel Corner. Pierce came out with the last load of dry goods to be taken over a few moments after they stepped away from the van. The cabin they had in River Run was strictly to get the girls back on their feet, but they still had other women—their own women who hadn't been some of the prostitutes who had gotten beaten—and that still wanted to earn. Malice closed the back of the van and looked up into the sky. It was dusk, and he had told Adrianna he'd be back later tonight. He hadn't called and checked in on her because it had only been a few hours, and he certainly didn't want to seem like some kind of stalker motherfucker.

"You getting Dakota tonight, right?" Tuck asked and leaned against the side of the van. He reached inside his cut and grabbed a joint.

The music from the clubhouse blasted out of the open window, and he could hear the laughter of some of the club pussy filter out. "Nah, tomorrow night." He was glad he had been open with Adrianna right way. It was better this way seeing as Molly came to the cabin once a week to check on everyone. He didn't want Adrianna getting surprised when the women and Molly started talking. Dakota normally was brought up in those conversations, and pictures passed around. His son was the main reason he lived, and these feelings he had for Adrianna made him want to share that very important part of himself with her.

"It's been a few months now, but your boy is holding up okay?" Tuck asked and then took a drag out of his joint. "He seems happy the few times Molly's brought him to the club." Tuck exhaled.

"Yeah, he's doing really well. Molly's going to be enrolling him in preschool come the fall."

"He's turning four already?" Tuck asked surprised.

"Yeah, crazy shit, huh?"

Tuck, Pierce, and Rock grunted.

"His birthday is coming up right before enrollment, so he is all excited about that."

"Damn, just starting out in the world." Rock had a joint between his lips and shook his head. "I swear I remember my first day of preschool."

"Get the fuck out of here," Tuck said and started laughing around his joint.

"Hey, don't laugh. I can remember my preschool years." Rock looked up at the sky. "Best fuckin' time of my life." He looked at them again. "Back then they had naps and snack and shit."

Malice started laughing, too. It felt good to have humor and not have this stick in his ass all the time. And the truth was he had been a grumpy asshole over the whole Molly situation.

"How are things with you two?" Tuck asked, because he was always so damn inquisitive.

"Molly? I'm good. I was good when she wanted to start dating Stinger."

Tuck cocked a brow, inhaled from his joint, and continued to stare at Malice without saying anything.

"You were good when she started dating Stinger?" Rock repeated what Tuck had said, and then chuckled.

"Fuck you."

"Hey, man, I thought I heard you and the Grizzly MC member went at it? Like went all primal in the woods behind the fight barn?" Pierce was outright howling with laughter now.

Malice was annoyed, but Pierce was right. "Listen, I thought I still loved her. I mean she's the mother of my kid for fuck's sake. But it wasn't about that. I had my own issues, wanted things the way they had been for so long, because that was what was comfortable. She's in good hands with Stinger, though, and the Grizzly takes care of Dakota when I'm not there." Tuck handed over his joint, and Malice grabbed it and took a deep inhale. When he exhaled and handed it back to Tuck he glanced at Rock, who stood beside Pierce. "Besides, I want Adrianna." There as a moment of silence, and he saw the way Rock and Tuck looked at each other.

Malice held his hand out, and Tuck grinned as he handed him the joint again. Once he had taken a couple of puffs and a nice buzz settled in, he realized that he had already known that Tuck and Rock had probably already caught on. They had been with him the entire time, and he knew it wasn't like he had hidden his reaction to Adrianna. He handed the joint back to Tuck and leaned against the van.

"What is this with her, a sex thing?" Rock asked.

Malice looked over at the other man and narrowed his eyes, but Rock held a hand up in surrender.

"Okay, not a sex thing. Shit." Rock looked ahead and finished smoking his joint. "'Cause I was going to say if it was a sex thing that is kind of fucked up, man." Rock looked back over at him. "I mean, given what she has been through."

"I said I wanted her at the meeting, didn't I?"

Rock shrugged. "Man, you were desperate to make sure she was taken care of. I probably would have said anything, too."

"She's different from anything I've ever felt before, and I feel very protective and possessive of her."

"No shit." Tuck was squinting at him through the haze of marijuana smoke. "You went all territorial with Kink, and then it was clear you had a hard-on for her back at Marx's." Before Malice could lay into Tuck about taking about that shit Tuck started speaking again. "And then you fucking laid claim on her. I meant no disrespect when I say that, by the way."

"Yeah, the whole fucking club knew that you wanted that woman for more than just a charity case, and that was before you said you wanted her as an old lady." Rock said, and Malice looked over at him. Rock shrugged.

Malice ran his fingers through his hair and tugged at the short strands at the nape of his neck. But he didn't say anything, and in fact had known that acting so barbaric and snapping at his Brothers wouldn't go unnoticed.

"So you're serious about her being your old lady?" Rock asked.

"Really fucking serious," Malice said and looked at each of them.

Malice looked at Tuck and narrowed his eyes.

"You can scowl at me all you want, man. You don't scare me." Tuck dropped his roach to the ground, snubbed it out, and then picked up the butt. He glanced at Malice and grinned.

Malice ground his teeth and pushed off the van. Tuck smiled, but it was a cocky and self-righteous one.

"Fuck, man, be careful because her life hasn't been a fairytale," said Tuck.

"You don't need to fucking tell me how her life has been. I was right fucking there." His anger was totally misplaced, and snapping at Tuck like this wasn't right, but the asshole was baiting him, and Malice knew why. They stood nearly toe-to-toe now, Malice breathing

MALICE'S POSSESSION

heavily as his anger was still very strong inside of him, and Tuck standing there with a stoic expression on his face.

"You're right, I don't need to tell you shit, but look at yourself, Malice." Tuck took a step back and did a onceover. "You're about a second away from kicking my fucking ass, and over what, because I said her life wasn't a fairytale? Or because I'm busting your balls?" Malice closed his eyes, loosened his hands that were in tight fists, and breathed. He realized that he had been having this internal fight with himself. And he didn't even know why.

"You want her, that's pretty fucking clear, but don't get fucking pissed when someone points out the obvious."

Malice started pacing, trying to calm down with every step he took. "It isn't just me wanting her more than I've ever wanted anyone before. It's that I feel like she knows me, like she doesn't judge me or my lifestyle. That's why I placed my claim with her at the meeting, and want her as my old lady." Yeah, she had mentioned he looked hard and scary, but she had still gone to him, still poured her heart out, and fuck, he was falling hard for this woman.

"Up until you met her you were all about the club whores."

He looked at Rock. "Yeah, and? You fuck these club girls after saying one syllable to them. Is it so hard to believe that I might want a woman for myself?"

"Sex doesn't equal love."

He turned on Rock and felt that familiar warmth of anger start to rise. He might not be in love with her yet, but fucking hell, he cared about that girl so damn much it consumed every part of him. If this was how he felt after only knowing her for such a short time, he didn't doubt he could love her so fucking hard it hurt.

Rock tilted his head toward the front door of the clubhouse. "If I asked you to come with me and pick out a fine looking honey to screw, would you go for it?"

Instantly Malice grew disgusted, because thinking about any other woman, about what they tasted like, smelled liked, and felt like under his mouth, tongue and hands turned him off faster than a cold shower.

"That's what I thought." Rock went to move past him, but smacked him on the back and said, "You want her, and if she wants you then go fucking take what's yours." And with that Rock moved away from them and into the clubhouse.

"He better not get shitfaced because he's taking this load over there tonight." Tuck grinned and moved over to him. He placed a hand on his shoulder, and the smell of the pot they just smoked, and whatever whiskey Tuck had been drinking on filled his nose. "I wasn't trying to bust your balls or start shit. I can tell you want this woman, and I'm glad you've found someone that draws you in like she does. You were with Molly for a long time, and I know sometimes it's hard to move on."

"No, I've moved on from Molly, as in when she told me it was over with. I was just too pigheaded and controlling to just let things end with the mother of my son. There weren't any real emotions between us for a long time before things ended."

"I know, but after that you were a cranky and foul bastard."

Malice chuckled, and then so did Tuck. "You going to the barn fight tonight?"

Tuck shook his head. "Kink's going." Tuck gave him a look that said Kink needed to blow off even more steam. The Brothers of Menace helped The Grizzly MC, a grizzly bear shifting MC that lived in Steel Corner, by fighting at the barn The Grizzlies ran. The underground bareknuckle fights brought in a little extra income to the club, but also allowed them to blow off some much needed steam.

They gave each other a half hug, and then Tuck turned away and headed toward the clubhouse. He stopped right before he entered and turned to look at him.

"You wanna throw back some drinks?"

Malice shook his head. "Nah. I'm heading out for the night." The look Tuck gave him told Malice that he knew he was going to see Adrianna. Tuck grinned and turned and headed inside. Malice stood there for a moment, thinking about all of the things Rock and Tuck had said and everything he had thought about and felt since he had met Adrianna. He was going to have her because there was no way he could stay away now. But she wanted him, too, and that was a pretty powerful fucking feeling. His cell vibrated in his pocket and he reached in and got it out. The screen flashed MOLLY. It wasn't who had been consuming his mind lately.

"Hey, what's up?" He held the cell to his ear and grabbed his keys for his bike and started moving toward the Harley.

"I'm going to have to cancel you getting Dakota tomorrow. He's got some kind of bug. He's been throwing up, as a little fever, and is as crabby as you are on most days." There was clear weariness in her voice.

"He's okay though? He doesn't need to see a doctor?" He was worried, but seeing as Molly was a nurse and trained in shit like this, Malice didn't freak out too badly.

"He's fine. There is some kind of crap going around the playground in town, and I am sure that is where he picked it up at."

"You want me to come over and see him? I can bring some soup over."

"You made soup?" Molly started chuckling, and Malice grunted.

"Fuck no, I didn't make soup, but Tatum made some chicken and rice this afternoon."

"No, but thank you. He can't keep much down and has been sleeping most of the day. He was disappointed in not seeing you, but I think it is best. You'd end up getting it, and then everyone would have to hear you bitch and moan." Molly started laughing again, and Malice could hear Stinger saying something in the background.

"Okay, but I'll call tomorrow and see how he is doing." There was a second of this weird silence, and Malice sighed. "What, Molly?"

"I was at the cabin in the back when you stopped by."

"Yeah." He straddled his bike, and although he didn't say it he knew what she was going to say.

"And I talked to the new girl … Adrianna."

He didn't respond, just put his helmet on anxious to get off the phone and see Adrianna. He wanted to see Dakota, but his kid's health came first, and if Molly thought he needed his rest, then he did.

"Some of the girls were talking about how you were the one to bring her to the cabin, and that she was staying there for an undetermined amount of time."

"Yeah, and? You've never questioned anything like this before, and some of the other guys brought women to the cabin."

"Yeah, but I also have never heard any of the other members doing inappropriate things with those women either."

Everything inside of Malice stilled. "Inappropriate things? What the fuck are you talking about?"

"Mandi said she was outside the bedroom door and heard a lot of moaning." There was a moment silence from Molly, and then he heard her sigh. "I don't care what you do, Malice, and as long as no one gets hurt and is happy is all that matters. But I saw Adrianna, spoke to her even. She's a sweet woman, but her life has been really screwed up. I can't help but think that doing sexual things with her in the mindset that she is in and especially after what had happened to her is not the best move."

Malice scratched his jaw and breathed out. "It isn't like that, Molly. I'm not attacking the poor girl because I'm hard-up. We..." He didn't even feel like getting into this with her, and it wasn't her damn business, and he was pissed that people had run their fucking mouths on shit they didn't know.

"You didn't have sex with an abuse victim?"

"Goddammit, Molly." He raised his voice, and although he didn't mean to yell at her the fact she was implying he had fucking done something wrong pissed him off. Malice heard Stinger's angry voice through the receiver. "Tell Stinger to calm the fuck down." He rubbed his eyes and listened to Molly calm down the other biker. "I don't have to explain myself to you or anyone else. I'm not some damn pervert that likes doing shit with women that are not consensual, or even implying that if she did do something with me it was because she was traumatized." He was pissed now, and as much as he meant what he said to Molly he had thought about wanting Adrianna as wrong because of what she had been through.

"Calm down, Trevor." Molly used his first name because she was pissed. That was the only time she ever did. "I'm not implying you're a pervert or a bad man. I am just asking that you be careful. Adrianna was really enamored with you, and the more we talked, and the more she was saying you saved her the more I realized that you could hurt her—"

There was that fucking word again … enamored. "I would never hurt her, Molly. I don't hurt women. Besides, Adrianna is different. I feel different when I'm around her." He didn't even want to be having this conversation with Molly but it was clear she was looking out for the other woman. "She's special." Another second of silence but he was done with this conversation. "Listen, I have to go. Thank you for looking out for her, and for wanting to make sure she was safe. That's what I want, too."

"You really care about her?"

"Yeah, Molly, I really do. And before you say how crazy it sounds I'll remind you that you and Stinger hadn't exactly been dating for years." No, they'd had pretty much jumped right into a relationship. If it feels right, and makes someone happy who the fuck cared how fast everything happened. "I really do have to go, but give Dakota a hug and kiss for me, and let him know I'll call him tomorrow to see how he is doing." After he disconnected the call he shoved the cell back in his cut and stare at the road in front of him. Of course Molly had brought up some good points, but that didn't mean they were real. He cared for Adrianna, and he knew she did as well. Did he think maybe she was drawn to him because he saved her? Maybe, but she was an adult, had lived a life that had made her realize what was real and what wasn't, and he had felt how genuine her words and touches had been.

"Fuck." He cursed feeling annoyed and irritated. The sun was just starting to set, and he watched it dip down past the horizon. Maybe if he wasn't such a selfish bastard he could have turned away from her, but they definitely had a connection, and besides, he couldn't get her off his brain. Starting the engine of his bike and revving the engine he sat there for only a second longer before pulling out onto the street. He'd find out how she really felt, but he'd also tell her that she was more to him that just someone to fuck.

## Chapter Fifteen

Adrianna cleaned off the stove and glanced at Malice's ex-girlfriend and the mother of his child. Molly handed the last washed dish to Kendra. Kendra was younger than Adrianna but not by much. She may have only been here for a day, but already she was feeling in her element and able to connect with these women. These women were like her, and they had all fallen into the same stereotypical life where they sold themselves for money, and allowed men to hurt them because that was the only kind of love they knew. But what set them apart, and what made them rise above the disgust and pain that had covered each of them was that they were here trying to get their lives back on track. Some may decide they wanted to continue to sell themselves while others went the more traditional route.

"So you're really thinking of going back to school?" Adrianna turned and glanced at Kendra. The other woman was drying the dish thoroughly, and when she opened the cabinet and placed it with the rest there was this smile on her face.

Molly excused herself to help one of the women that had fallen down the last few stairs and had hurt her ankle.

"I'm thinking about it, but I am scared to be honest," Kendra said and turned to face Adrianna.

"That's normal."

"Yeah?"

Adrianna tossed the rag she had been cleaning with in the hamper with the rest of the dirty clothes. "Sure. If you weren't scared of something new then I would wonder if it was the right thing or not."

Kendra smiled and looked down. "Yeah, I hope you're right."

Kendra was still very young in the mentality stage. She was beautiful and intelligent, but Adrianna could still see why the horrible men in her life had taken advantage of her. She was delicate, like a flower just opening up to the world. They had spoken a lot today, and just in these last twenty-four hours Adrianna had realized that she was glad life had taken her here. Someone called out for Kendra, and she smiled once more at Adrianna before heading out of the kitchen. There were still a few women that kept their distance from her, but she was the "new girl", and she supposed living the life they all had made them prone to be wary of others they didn't know.

She moved over to the kitchen table and sat down. There were still some spaghetti sauce spots on the table from the group dinner they had just had. All Adrianna could think about as she stared at those spots was the conversation she had with Molly just today. She had known Malice had been with someone before, and knew he had a kid. She had also known that Molly had been his, and although Arianna had never been jealous, because, well, she didn't have much in life to be jealous of, she was envious of this woman that had shared her life with such a wonderful man. On the heels of those misplaced feelings she also felt guilt and shame. Molly had been so kind, so caring, and had talked with each of the women. Kendra especially seemed close with Molly, and then when Adrianna spoke with the other women, everything just kind of opened up. Even now she remembered the warmth that had come from Molly, and how it had been like nothing Adrianna had ever felt.

*"You have to do what is best for you."* She reached out and placed her hand over Adrianna's. *"The women here talk, but that is just what women do."* Molly smiled. *"You care for Malice, and I can see that. He is a*

*great guy, a wonderful father, and is loyal right down to his heart." Molly squeezed Adrianna's hand gently. "But don't settle for what you are not ready for, just because he is the first man to offer you that shred of hope. Sometimes it is not, and I don't say this to dissuade you from following what you know is right and true. Just know that only you can decide what is moving too fast or too slowly."*

Adrianna blinked, knowing that she could see how an outsider would feel that the life she had led made her feel the things she did for Malice. Although she had wanted to talk more with Molly, the woman was here to help all of the girls, and that took time. She wasn't just there to tend to wounds, but to be that shoulder these women needed to lean on. Maybe soon she and Molly could speak more, a little more in-depth, and Adrianna could really find out about her and Malice. It wasn't just about wanting more from him than what she had. He was her savior, this knight in shining armor that had helped her when the world was dark. But this had nothing to do with the abuse by Phillip, or the death of her brother, or her shitty home life. This was about taking a stand and deciding that now was the time for her to take something for herself.

She stood when she heard the front door open, and then her heart started to race when she heard the women greet Malice. The sound of his heavy boots hitting the floor came closer, and then there he was. He stood in the doorway looking like it had been years since he had seen her. Emotions swamped her, and adrenaline flooded her veins in sweet release. All she had to do to know this is the right thing was look in his ruggedly handsome face.

"I sent a text to tell you I was on my way."

That scratchy husky voice of his always had the same effect in her: made her wet in a matter of seconds. "I left the phone upstairs."

He nodded and then looked over at the stairs. "Can we talk someplace privately?"

Instantly her arousal dimmed at the tone of his voice. "Okay." She moved toward the entryway of the kitchen, and she swore she heard him inhale as she passed. Her arm brushed against his chest, and she felt that flutter of excitement in her belly. They moved through the living room where many of the women were gathered around the television. Adrianna didn't miss the curious glances they gave her, but she had also heard the whispers of their suspicions. Yes even after one day she was the talk of the house. Once they were in her room she shut the door and pressed her back to it. Malice stood in the center staring out her window. He was so big and imposing that he made everything in the room seem so small and insignificant.

"What's on your mind?"

He slowly turned around, and she took in the full scope of him. Black scuffed up boots, jeans that looked worn-in and used, but only in the best kind of way, plain black t-shirt that showed off the sleeves of his tattoos on his arms, and of course his leather biker vest. His dark hair fell slightly across his cheeks, and he had yet to shave. Adrianna liked the trimmed beard on him though. It gave him a very rugged appearance and made his masculinity even more pronounced.

"You're on my mind."

Her pulse increased and moved up her throat. Those words might not have meant much to someone else, but to her they meant so much more.

"You spoke with Molly today?" he asked.

Of course she wasn't surprised that he knew about her conversation with Molly. She was the mother of his child after all. "Yeah, earlier today. She's a very sweet woman and cares about these girls."

He nodded and glanced away. He didn't say anything for several seconds, and she started to feel like the calm before the storm. Was he about to say something bad?

"She's worried about you."

A relieved breath left her. "Yeah, I got that from our conversation, but I think it is in her nature to worry about others. Besides, these other women have had such a crummy hand dealt to them."

"So have you."

She shrugged. She couldn't deny it, but she didn't want to play the victim or look like one either.

"She thinks maybe you and me shouldn't go down this road because of what happened to you." He rubbed the back of his neck in what she knew was an uncomfortable gesture. "She thinks that you see me as your rescuer and that is why you have these feelings for me."

Her cheeks heated instantly, and she didn't even know why. For a moment she didn't know what to say. Of course she had thought those same things, but in the end she knew that wasn't just why she cared about him. It was a part of it, but not the entire reason. "Is that what you think?"

He stared at her, not responding right away, and this dread settled into her belly. "The thought did cross my mind."

Adrianna nodded, not knowing what to say to that.

"But it doesn't change how I feel for you, and the fact that the way you look at me, open up to me when we talk, and are so fucking receptive to my touches, that make me realize that I'm not alone in this." He took step toward her. "But I want you to know *why* you want me and that it isn't because the life you had was hard. I want to be able to protect you, make sure you are always safe, and never afraid of anything again." He stared at her hard and unyielding. "I want you as my old lady. Do you understand what that means?"

*Yes and no.* She swallowed roughly, on the verge of tears because his words pierced right through her heart like a spear. She had heard some of the women talking about how none of the bikers had old ladies, and Adrianna had to assume that was what the MC called their girlfriends. But for some reason she thought that the term as an old lady meant a hell of a lot more than just being a girlfriend, or even a wife. "What I feel for you has nothing to do with my past, or that I am afraid of what the future holds. Yes, all of this is fast, but who cares? I know what I feel and that all of it is genuine and true." She waited for him to say something, anything, but he kept quiet and took another step forward. "And I have a feeling I know what an old lady really means." When he was right in front of her all she could do was inhale the scent that was sweet and spicy, and had a hint of darkness to it. "This is what I want, Malice." She stared up at him, tired of trying to hold herself back from what she wanted—from what she deserved. And then he had his hands on either side of her face and his mouth on hers. After that Adrianna was lost to the sensations crashing through her at an astounding rate.

****

Malice wanted to go softly, to make sure she was with him one-hundred percent. But when she gripped his biceps and dug her nails into his skin, something snapped inside of him. Her words played over and over in his head, and he couldn't help but feel the possessiveness and proprietary nature inside of him grow. From the moment he saw her he knew she was his, and that he would kill anyone else that thought about fucking that up.

He stroked the seam of her lips with his tongue until she opened her mouth, and then he delved inside, fucking her with the muscles until these breathy little sounds escaped her. For several minutes all they did was kiss, and the sounds she made fueled his own, had his cock hard as steel and were playing havoc with his self-control. He broke the kiss, sucked in air, and immediately started trailing his lips and tongue along her jaw-line. You want this as much as I do, Adrianna." He had since moved his hands down to her shoulders, and he pulled her closer. She smelled so fucking good, sweet and floral, and he grew drunk from the aroma.

"I want this, Malice." He could feel her letting her head fall back slightly, and he used that as an opportunity to suck and lick at the spot right below her ear. Her pulse was beating hard beneath his tongue, and he sucked her flesh into his mouth, not caring if he left a mark. In fact, he *wanted* to leave a mark on her.

He groaned against her throat, and he felt her tremble beneath his hands. The possessive side of him rose up, wanting to make sure she knew that he would never let her go, and never let her be in pain again. "Fuck, I want you so badly. I want to make you mine, make you scream my name, and have you cry out for more." He moved his hands between their bodies to cup her breasts. They were full, pressing against the material of her shirt and spilling over the top. He squeezed the mounds, gave a low growl, and slipped his fingers under the hem of the fabric. He skimmed his fingers along her bare flesh, loved that her skin was slightly damp from sweating because she was so turned on, and forced himself to go slow. But he had never been the kind of man that had patience, especially not when he wanted Adrianna this badly. He slid his hand up the center of her chest, and when he felt the swell of her breast something inside of him snapped He wrenched her shirt up and over her head, and stared down at her chest. The heavy, big mounds were barely contained in her bra, but he wanted that gone, too.

When he tore the bra from her body and her breasts sprang free and shook from the force. He was losing it as he stared at her chest, watched as the red tipped peaks hardened even further, and knew that what he felt for this woman wasn't just for this one night. Even after he had her, had placed his claim on her by pounding his dick in and out of her, and hearing her call out his name, he wouldn't be able to stop. He needed more of her, all of her, and judging by the way she looked at him, and how she reacted to his touches, Malice knew she wanted this just as much. She was his, and he had known that from the moment he saw her.

## Chapter Sixteen

Adrianna couldn't breathe, couldn't even see straight as she stared at Malice. She stood before him with only her pants on, but there was no chill moving through her. All she felt was this intense heat, and the longer he stared at her the more powerful it became. Before she could say anything, if she could even form the right words, he was right in front of her. His breath smelled good, like mint and cinnamon combined. He reached out, cupped her bare flesh with both of his hands, and squeezed to the point of pain. She didn't want foreplay, though. All Adrianna wanted was to feel Malice over her, sliding in and out of her body with all of that raw power he held, and making her forget—even for a small window of time—the pain she had lived. No more thinking, no more questioning and worrying about what she should and shouldn't do. That had never helped her in life, and this moment was something she desperately wanted. *Malice* was what she desperately wanted.

He took her mouth again in a brutal kiss, and she swore she could feel him in every part of her. It was like he wasn't only just touching her breasts and stroking his tongue with hers. Not breaking the kiss, she reached between them and started working the button and zipper of his jeans down. He didn't stop her, and instead groaned against her. Taking his hand from one of her breasts was disappointing, but when he spread his fingers through her hair and cupped the back of her head, she grew even more pliant. Once his pants were off he took a step back. God, he hadn't even been wearing any underwear. That realization had her clenching her thighs together as more wetness spilled from her. But it was the sight of the piercing at the tip of his dick that stunned, frightened, and aroused her. It was a curved silver barbell, intimidating and like nothing she had ever seen in person before. He was huge between his thighs, but then again he was a big man all over. But seeing it, confined by nothing, pierced and standing straight and hard between his thighs, had her whole body tensing with arousal. He even had a pearl sized drop of pre-cum dotting the tip, and that had a wave of heat filling her. Never had she felt such potent desire for another person, but then again she had never felt the kind of things that she felt for Malice with anyone else.

He gripped his shaft and stroked the massive length several times while watching her. It seemed vulgar and obscene, but God she loved it, and loved watching him do it. But it was when he took off his cut, placed it on the dresser, and then removed his shirt that she had to clench her hands into fists by her sides to stop herself from reaching out and touching him. She wanted him, wanted to run her tongue along all of the hard muscle on his body, and over the tattoos that covered it. Seeing Malice with no clothes on and clearly wanting her was an aphrodisiac all in itself. He had a very light sprinkling of hair on his upper chest, and a dark line of hair that started at his belly button and went right down to his cock. And when he had turned she had seen the tattoo on his back. It was the same patch design of the one he wore on his cut: a motorcycle silhouetted behind a rising phoenix. With his arms and chest covered in ink, he looked so good, so dangerous, and so very masculine. In his presence she felt like a woman. He moved back toward her, slid his hands down her collarbones, across her breasts, and continued his path until he got to her pants. He didn't remove them right away like she would have thought, but instead rested his head in the crook of her neck. Seconds passed that felt more like minutes, and all she wanted was to do this, to finally feel him do the things to her that she envisioned. They may have only known each other for such a short time, but when something felt this good it seemed almost wrong to go against it.

"Why are you stopping?" She could hear her pulse racing in her ears, and feel it in her throat.

"Are you sure about this, baby, because once we do this it can't be undone." His voice was so very deep, and she felt it vibrate along her neck. "When I take you it will be for good, I will not let you go. I'll make sure everyone knows you're my old lady, and that if they fuck with you, they fuck with me." He breathed in and out heavily, and his warm, humid breath was making another part of her even moister. "And believe me when I say they don't want to fuck with me and what's mine."

She had no doubts that he could deliver on that promise. Hell, she had seen his fierceness already. She shook her head and lifted her hands so she could rest them on his narrow waist. "I'm sure. I don't think I have ever been surer of anything in my life before." And she meant that, every single word. She heard him swallow, and then when she moved her hands up his sides and rested them on his pecs he groaned. When he moved closer and the hot, hard length of his cock pressed against her belly, a half sigh half moan left her. A spark of iciness touched her skin, and she looked down and stared at the piercing at the tip of his erection. She knew enough that that type of piercing was called a Prince Albert. Of course she couldn't help but wonder how it would feel inside of her.

"I want you so fucking badly." He breathed against her, groaned and thrust his hips forward so she felt his cock and piercing once again. "I could come without even being inside of you, baby." He ran his tongue up the length of her throat. "I could lick every part of you, suck at your nipples, your clit…"

A tremble moved through her, and she tightened her hands on his shoulders

"I could suck on you all night long until you came all over my face." He scraped his teeth over the area he had just run his tongue along. "I want to memorize you, Adrianna, so that there isn't one inch of you that isn't ingrained in my head."

She felt dizzy, high, and drunk from the sensation overload that was swarming her. "*Please*, Malice."

He groaned against her neck, but he didn't kiss her or touch her anymore. Instead he pulled back so they were looking into each other's eyes. "Hold on, baby." He pulled away from her, and she braced a hand on the wall beside her for support.

Her knees shook, her head spun, and she was so uncomfortably wet that she wanted out of her panties and pants. Everything felt hazy, but soon her mind and vision cleared and she was able to focus on what Malice was doing: grabbing a condom. She clenched her thighs together once more because the sight of his wide shoulders and muscular back covered in ink had her clit tingling. He turned back around, and of course her gaze went right to the massive cock that jutted from him. But Adrianna couldn't help it.

He stalked forward, and really there was no other word that effectively described what he was doing. He stopped mere inches from here, and she stared at the small cut on his bottom lip. Without thinking, just acting, she lifted her hand and ran the pad of her finger right beside it. He didn't move, didn't even flinch. He just stared right into her eyes.

"Do I frighten you?" he said low and then glanced down at her mouth.

"A little." There was no need to lie, but even if she said no Adrianna knew he would have known she was lying.

He lifted his hand and ran his thumb along her bottom lip. "Your instincts are telling you I am not a good man." He was focused on what he was doing with his thumb on her lip. "You're smart to be afraid of me, but you," he lifted his gaze to hers, "shouldn't be. Ever." He slipped his hand behind her head, tangled his fingers in her hair, and leaned down to kiss her. With his lips still on hers he moved forward, which caused her to move backward. The edge of the bed stopped her from moving any further.

"You're so fucking gorgeous, Adrianna." He started touching her all over now, and it was like an animal was unleashed. He covered her chest with his big hands and rubbed his thumbs along the aching peaks. He did this for long, agonizing minutes, and just when she opened her mouth to tell him she couldn't handle anymore, he slipped his hands down and in a matter of seconds had her pants and panties off.

There she stood, completely bared for him, and never before feeling this kind of heat and chill move through her body at the same time. She opened her mouth, but no words came out. Malice made this low sound in his throat, and in the next second he was gripping her ass and lifting her up. On instinct she wrapped her legs around his waist and her arms around his neck. Her breasts were pressed snugly against his muscular chest, and the solid, hot length of his cock slid through her slick folds. He rubbed his beard covered cheek along her smooth one, and the scruff abraded her flesh in the most delicious ways. And then she was on her back on the bed with Malice over her. He used his narrow hips to push her thighs apart, and the stretch of unused muscles protested from the action.

"Malice." She hadn't meant to say his name, but it had come from her on its own, as if she were pleading for him to give her what she really needed.

"I know, baby. I fucking know what you need, because it's what I need, too." His cock was steel against her pussy, and the thick length slid along her folds and parted them. The cold and hard ridge from his piercing teased her overheated skin. A groan spilled from her, and she was surprised by how needy sounding it was.

"I want you, Malice." She didn't know what had gotten into her, but she didn't want to stop. He leaned down and nuzzled her at the same time he ground his cock into her. The base of his shaft pressed into her clit, sending sparks of electricity through her. "Christ, baby, you have no idea how good that feels." He pressed more firmly against her, and her mouth opened on a silent cry. He kept hold of her with one strong hand, and used the other to reach between their bodies and align the tip of his dick with the opening of her body. Adrianna wasn't a virgin, but she also hadn't been with a man that was so well endowed. His gaze was trained between them, and the fact that he was watching himself as he pushed his dick into her body was so damn erotic. He closed his eyes, clenched his jaw, and said, "You're so fucking wet for me." He moved the tip up and down her slit, and then pushed just the tip into her. "And so *tight*." He said the last word on a groan. "If you knew how hard I want to fuck you, how much I want you to feel that you're mine, I'd frighten you, baby."

Adrianna closed her eyes close at the delicious way he stretched her and at the feeling of his piercing hidden only by a thin layer of latex moving against her sensitive flesh. "God, Malice, I want that." She felt delirious for him and loved his filthy words. The burning pain and ecstasy slammed into her as he continued to push all of those long, thick inches inside of her. The pain left her as the pleasure increased. He moved his hands behind her and gripped her ass in a bruising hold. She liked that added spark of pain, loved that it told her he was barely controlling himself.

"You're so fucking tight and hot." His voice was guttural, and his eyes were closed. With every inch he pushed into her, she finally realized what it was to be claimed. She had never felt this way about anyone, had never even thought feeling these emotions and sensations was possible. "Does it feel good, baby?" he asked in a harsh voice.

"Yes. God, it feels so good."

With one more thrust he buried the last inch of his cock into her and groaned out deeply. They both let out a hard grunt of pleasure, and Adrianna curled her nails into his back, loving how he filled and stretched every single part of her. He pulled out of her, and then pushed back in just as slowly. His breath became quicker when he started thrusting in and out of her, and the heavy sack beneath his dick slapped against her ass.

"Oh my God, Malice." She felt her eyes widen, knew her orgasm was imminent, and tightened her hold on him.

"That's it." He groaned out. "Dig your nails into me. Make it fucking hurt, baby."

It was agony and ecstasy all rolled into one. With every thrust of his hips she moved up on the bed, but he placed a hand on her shoulder and kept her stationary for his erotic punishment. A high pitched gasped left her. "More, Malice. God, *more*." Here she was, begging him for it harder and faster. He never stopped his steady thrusting. In and out, and more ferociously. He lowered his head, and his mouth was right by her ear. She tightened her hold on him, wanting him closer, because for this one moment Malice didn't want anyone but her.

"God, I've never felt anything like this, Adrianna." His voice was a rough whisper. The root of his cock rubbed along her clit, back and forth, again and again until that burst of pleasure escalated.

Her entire body tightened, signaling her climax. The pleasure rushed to the surface and stole all of her sanity. "I'm close, Malice." His name came out of her on a gasp.

"Come all over my cock, baby." He thrust hard and severely into her, hitting something deep that had her inner muscles clenching around him violently. "Yeah, that's fucking it. Tighten around me, make me come right along with you, Adrianna."

Adrianna arched her neck and opened her mouth on a silent cry. Her climax took everything out of her, stole her energy, her strength, and replaced it with this euphoric sensation. He slammed into her, pressing his body fully against hers now as he continued to pump his hips back and forth. Her thighs ached from how wide they were spread, and her skin was slick with perspiration. He bottomed out in her, almost slipped free from her body, but then just as quickly slammed back into her. He was an animal as he made these guttural noises and nipped at her neck. When her orgasm started to wane he reached between their bodies and found her clit with his thumb.

"Come on, baby. Don't make me work for a second one," he grunted out. "Make my dick good and wet." It was like he knew the pleasure was ebbing and wasn't about to have any of that.

"I want to fuck you so hard, make you scream out my name." He pounded into her harder now, and a cry of pain and pleasure left her. "I want to do filthy fucking things to you, lick every part of your body, and then slide my dick into your tight ass."

His word were so coarse and hard, but they matched the way he was fucking her, and that was exactly what he was doing. Another orgasm slammed into her so fast that stars danced in front of her vision. She was about to cry out again, but Malice anticipated it and slammed his mouth on hers so hard their teeth clashed together. Her lips would be sore, but she didn't care. Spearing her hands in his hair, she tugged on the strands and moaned.

"But all of that can wait, because right now this is all I want, Adrianna. *You* are all I want." With one more brutal push into her Malice buried his entire length in her pussy and groaned out as he came. She swore she could feel him swell even further, and feel the heavy pulse as he emptied himself. When he sagged against her, his chest rising and falling, compressing hers and causing it to be difficult for her to breathe, she closed her eyes and sighed. He clenched the hand still holding onto her ass cheek and groaned once more. "Shit, Adrianna. That was…"

When he didn't respond she opened her eyes and turned her head so she could look at him. "Yeah, I know what you mean."

He braced his elbow on the bed by her head and pushed up slightly. He used his other hand to brush away her bangs. For several seconds neither said anything, but it was a very comfortable silence. The sounds of music and laughter came from the main room, but it seemed so distant, and as if they were in a different world.

"Everything is going okay here?"

She curled into him more and closed her eyes, just absorbing his scent and body heat. "It is. Honestly, these women are very strong, and are already talking about the things they want out of life."

He ran his fingers up and down her arm. "It takes a strong woman to survive things like they have ... like you have." He leaned down and kissed the crown of her head.

"I overheard some of them talking about working with Lucien and the club once they are ready."

He hummed in agreement in a very sleepy way. "It's their choice what they want to do. If they want to go back to selling themselves, that's their choice. We can hire them to work for the club doing that. They will be safe and protected. But if they want to do other things, cleaning, cooking, shit like that, we can help find them something as well."

She closed her eyes, thinking over everything he had said, and all the things she had experienced while in River Run.

"How do you honestly feel about me being in the MC and how we make a living?"

She leaned back and looked at him in the face. How did she feel? "Honestly?" She stared at him, and then he nodded. Before she answered she lifted her hand and ran her finger between his eyes. His entire body shook as if he couldn't control himself, and she realized a man of this size and power was just as breakable as she was. "Honestly, it doesn't bother me." She smiled and pushed his hair away from his face. She ran her fingers over his beard, loved that the short coarse strands tickled her skin, and sighed. "I have been around illegal and immoral things my entire life, and none of them had been anywhere near this kind of set-up." She glanced at the ceiling and let her gaze travel over the natural pine structure and beams. "You actually care, as does your club. These women are going to sell themselves no matter what." When she looked at Malice she could see he still had this hard look on his face.

"We do bad shit, too, Adrianna."

His body was strung so tight that she could feel the clench and unclenching of his muscles under her hands. "We all have done bad shit in our lives." Did she want to know every little thing that made up Malice? One day, yes, but right now she was content with the man he had showed her. "You know, when I first started dating Phillip he was nice and sweet, a real gentleman." The low sound that came from Malice was very hostile, but she felt no fear from it. "But even though he showed me this really great guy on the outside, I knew deep down he was no different from the men my mother always hung around."

"Why did you stay with him?"

She shrugged, still feeling shame and self-disgust that she hadn't been stronger and that she allowed herself to be subjected to that. "I don't know. Maybe I thought I didn't deserve better."

"I don't ever want to fucking hear you say that again." His tone was hard and brooked no argument, and she was seeing that strong biker that didn't take shit from anyone break through.

"You're right, Malice. I shouldn't allow myself to think like that." This was a long road for her, but she knew she didn't want to do it alone. "But even though I fell for Phillip's façade I also believe that I have grown stronger from everything that has happened." He hadn't asked her about a detailed report of her past, and for that she was thankful for. Some things were meant to stay behind them.

"I'm not like that motherfucker."

Would she ever get used to his growly attitude? She didn't think so, but she liked it. It made her actually feel alive, and that was the first time she had ever said that or felt that way. "Believe me, I know that, *knew* that instantly."

He pulled her closer to him again, and she rested her head on his chest. The sun had already set, and although there was laughing downstairs, and it broke up the silence that surrounded them, there was this tranquility in her. If this was a bad mistake, then it was the best one she had ever made.

****

Adrianna stared out her bedroom window and watched some of the girls work on the garden outside.

"Do you want to talk about anything?"

Adrianna looked at Molly and shook her head. "Not really. Things have been going well, actually." Adrianna turned back around and stared at Kendra, who was laughing at something Cecilia said. The windows in the cabin were pretty thick, and so she didn't hear a car approaching until she saw the dark van with a massive cross making its way toward the cabin. But the Brothers that were there watching over them that day were already on it. There were no fences or gates around the property, because honestly unless someone knew about this place it was pretty much off the map.

Tuck and Pierce were here today, and they stood in front of the driveway, blocking the van from moving any closer. Two men climbed out of the vehicle, one from the driver's side, the other from the passenger side. For a moment they seemed to just be talking, but when of the guys handed Tuck a piece of paper she swore she could feel the blast of anger come from the biker. Tuck all but threw the paper back in the other guy's face, and when it was clear the van people were not moving, Tuck reached behind him, grabbed the gun that was tucked in the waistband of his pants at the small of his back, and pointed it at all men. The women working in the garden realized what was happening, and Pierce moved toward them and ushered them inside. Adrianna didn't move, and she watched as Tuck kept raising his hand that held the gun at the guys, and clearly shouting at them. Finally the guys climbed back in the van and backed out. She had no clue what that was all about, but she did know that Tuck, or any of the other bikers for that matter, didn't overreact about anything. They did things for a reason, and clearly those men in the van were a threat. She watched as Tuck got his phone out, and then he was bringing it to his ear and talking to someone as he moved toward the side of the cabin.

"Adrianna, everything okay?" Molly asked.

Adrianna turned away from the window and smiled. "Yeah." She wasn't going to let what was going on outside interfere with her talk with Molly, especially since if there was immediate danger Tuck would have gotten them away from the cabin.

"You like staying here?"

Adrianna nodded. "I just kind of feel out of place sometimes." She knew Molly was Malice's ex, but she was also the house nurse for the girls. This was the first time they had really talked since Adrianna had been calling the cabin home. She didn't know a whole lot personally about Molly, but what she did know was that the other woman was genuine, kind, and thought about others. She wished she would have had a friend like this while growing up. It might have made things easier and more bearable in her life. But she was glad Molly had come today and that Adrianna was finally opening up a little to her.

"But no one has made you feel that way, right?" There was genuine worry in Molly's voice, and for the first time since Malice had taken her out of the rain and back to that clubhouse, she felt like someone actually cared for her.

"No, they have been supportive, but some are apprehensive of my presence, but if I had lived their lives I would feel the same." She turned away from the window and sat beside Molly on the edge of the bed.

Molly reached out and held Adrianna's hand. "You have lived their life, Adrianna."

Although Adrianna hadn't sold her body, she had sold her life for a moment of happiness, and look where it had gotten her. There were a lot of things she wanted to talk about with Molly, about what would happen once this was all said and done, and about where she would go. Malice had told her not to worry, that everything would work out, but she couldn't help but think about how she would repay all of them for their kindness. And even though she did worry about all of that, she couldn't help but be curious about the life that Molly had led with Malice. The truth was she cared for the big brute of a biker. He was coarse and crude, but with her he was gentle, caring, and had gone above and beyond to leave her horrid life behind her. He had made sure she was safe, and a part of her saw him as this hero. He was *her* hero. "Can I ask you something?"

Molly smiled and nodded, and continued to hold her hand. "Of course."

It took Adrianna a minute to actually find the nerve to bring up Malice, because aside from the few conversations that they had where all they mentioned was Malice and Molly previously being a couple, no one mentioned their connection again. Maybe Adrianna should just bite her tongue, but honestly she wanted to know more about Malice. There was something about him that made her feel connected, safe, and wanted. "You and Malice used to be together?" God, she sounded so immature saying that. She knew they had been together, but she was hoping to build up to a more in-depth conversation regarding him.

Molly just smiled and patted her hand once before pulling it away. "We were together years ago, and have a wonderful little boy to show for it." Molly swallowed audibly, and Adrianna felt like a bitch for bringing it up since it seemed like Molly was uncomfortable.

"I'm sorry, I just…" Now it was her turn to swallow. "It's just Malice was the one to save me when I was at my lowest. I don't know where I would be without him."

"Honey, what you went through was traumatic. Of course you feel like he is your knight in shining armor." She smiled again. "Malice is good like that. He's a wonderful father and was a good significant other. It's just we weren't right for each other.

Moly shrugged and looked down at her hand. "I love Stinger, and being with him is where I feel is the perfect place for my heart." She smiled, but she still looked down at her hands. "Being with a man in a MC is a different life." When Molly looked at her then there was this seriousness covering her face. "It's a hard life, one that drains your guy to the bone, and they need a strong woman to hold them up and patch their wounds."

Adrianna nodded, and although she didn't speak about being with Malice as anything more than what they were, she also knew that Molly must have been able to hear the longing in her voice.

"Malice is a good man, a fabulous father, and is all about loyalty." Molly stared right into her eyes, as if willing her to understand what she was saying. "If he wants something then he doesn't stop until he gets it."

When Molly stopped speaking Adrianna took in her words, rolled them around in her head, and wanted to believe that he wanted her and that was why he had gone out of his way. Any physical connection that they had could strictly be because he was a man in need of a woman. Or maybe he felt like he had this connection with her, too, that he wanted to be with her like she wanted to be with him. It was hard, something she thought about a lot since she had woken up in that clubhouse, and one she hoped to explore. But it was frightening to say the least.

"Go with what feels right in here." Molly placed a hand over her heart. And when she smiled Adrianna knew that Molly could tell she wanted Malice in a way that was so much more. "Listen, I have a few other girls to check on, but if you ever need anything, or just want to talk you have my number." Molly stood and Adrianna did the same, and after she gave Adrianna a hug and Molly left she stood there and stared out the window. She took the few words Molly had said and let them register. Did she really want to go down that path with Malice? And if he wanted to go down that road with her was it going to be real?

## Chapter Seventeen

*Two weeks later*

It had only been fourteen days, and Adrianna felt strangely right at home at the cabin, but she also missed Malice. It might have been very fast that her feelings for him had escalated to this point, but she knew better than anyone that life could be snuffed out faster than she could blink. If she truly wanted him—which she did—she needed to embrace that and just go with it. Her physical wounds were already healed, and she loved being at the cabin and helping the other girls not only with domestic things, but also talking with them. Strangely she had a lot in common with them with bad childhoods, abusive relationships, and then finally finding her way to The Brothers of Menace cabin. These women might have been former prostitutes, and might even go back to doing that line of work when they decided they wanted to leave River Run, but Adrianna didn't judge. In fact she found that they had so much strength, were loving toward each other, and only wanted to survive in this world.

Adrianna wiped off the kitchen counter one last time. Everyone was gone for the evening. The women had taken Kendra into town, and she had heard from Tatum that they were all going to meet up at the clubhouse for a surprise and impromptu birthday party. Adrianna was spending the evening with Malice and his son, maybe even spending the night, but she planned on seeing Kendra on her birthday sometime tonight. No way would she miss that sweet girl's birthday. She closed her eyes and breathed out deeply. She may have only known the women a couple of weeks, but she considered them her family. They were women that had faced a lot of horrors: born from crack addicted mothers, sold to random men their fathers knew, and finally becoming the only thing they knew about. They were survivors; *she* was a survivor, and she reminded herself of that every day. They were furthering their education and living in a home provided to them by an outlaw motorcycle club. Her nerves were causing her hands to shake and her palms to sweat. She had yet to meet Dakota, and she did worry that the little boy wouldn't like her. Adrianna wasn't accustomed to being around children, and for that she was thankful, because the life she had been subjected to shouldn't have children involved anyway.

She looked at the clock and saw that Malice would be there to pick her up any minute, so she quickly put the cleaning supplies away and went to the foyer. The house was so still and silent with no one in it, empty in not just the literal sense. Working at the cabin allowed her to earn some money, and she was proud to have it saved away in a small bank account in town. Malice had even helped her get the five hundred dollars she had in the Fairview bank. Now she had a nice little nest egg, nothing extravagant, but enough that she felt somewhat secure knowing she had that back-up. Next on her list was getting herself a car, and maybe one day a home for herself, but to be honest she was thinking about Malice, and what it would be like to stay with him. Of course he had broached the subject of her moving in with him. It wasn't like they kept what they had a secret. Everyone knew their relationship started off complicated, but she wasn't going anywhere, and she knew in her heart that neither was Malice. He had said as much, and even though it had only been two weeks, being with him felt right on every single level.

This wasn't just a sexual relationship with Malice, although just thinking about his big, hard body over hers, cradling her, protecting her, and bringing her to the brink of death with the pleasure he gave her had her entire body heating. She was like a fiend for him, because it wasn't that he made her feel so incredibly good. It was the way he held her, talked to her and made sure she was okay, that made the experience more intimate.

She opened the front door, and something on the porch caught her attention. She glanced down, saw a piece of paper under a rock by the door, and bent down to pick it up. It was some kind of church pamphlet. "The Church of the Good and Only," she read out loud. The name sounded a little narrow-minded and pretentious. She turned and tossed the paper on the table by the door and stepped out and onto the patio. She shut the front door just as she heard Malice's Harley coming closer. Ruin and Rock had left about twenty minutes ago since they were the ones that took the ladies to town, but Pierce had stayed behind just until Malice showed up. Pierce came out of the small cabin to the side of the main one. It was for the guys to sleep when they were staying over and watching things. He waved to her just as Malice pulled his bike to a stop in front of her. She moved toward Malice and couldn't help but smile. God, she missed him.

"You ready, baby?" He grinned at her and reached out to pull her close. He kissed her long, hard, and slow. He was thorough as he kissed her, and she felt herself grow warm and wet, and so ready for him. She didn't even care that Pierce could see them.

"I'm more than ready." Molly was dropping Dakota off at Malice's house for a few hours. They'd have dinner, maybe watch a movie, and she'd have to try to win the little guy over.

Malice grinned and held out a helmet for her. Once she had it on and was straddling the powerful machine beneath her, she breathed in deeply. She wrapped her arms around his waist, and rested her cheek on his back. This was what freedom felt like, and it was the best damn feeling in the world. He went to pull away from the cabin, and she looked over to see Pierce doing the same thing, but then it was like time stilled. The massive explosion that destroyed the bikers' cabin had a pulse of energy moving outward. She was thrown off the back of the bike, and landed on the ground hard enough that stars danced in front of her vision. There was this loud ringing that filled her head, and when a large piece of debris landed right beside her she covered her head, despite having the helmet on. It seemed like forever that pieces of wood, metal, and other debris spilled out around her, and when she felt it was safe enough to move she looked up. Malice was moving toward her with angry, determined strides. He knelt beside her, black smudges on his face, and lifted his hands to remove his helmet.

"Baby, are you okay?"

She pushed herself up into a sitting position and nodded. "Yeah, just a little dizzy."

He helped her remove her helmet, and she started coughing as the thick, dark smoke started to billow around them. She stared at the burning cabin. "Oh my God. Pierce—"

Malice shook his head, stopping her from finishing. "He's scraped up, but alive."

She looked over his shoulder and saw Pierce moving toward them. He was slumping, but he was speaking in a clipped, hard tone to someone on the phone. Thank God he was alive. Thank God all of them were alive. Malice helped her up, and they moved farther away from the fire. The sound of sirens in the distance drowned out some of the crackling, popping wood as the fire licked at the building. The structure crumbled, and she screamed from surprise. Malice covered her body with his, and she felt him kiss the top of her head.

"Tuck said the girls are safe, and Lucien and the boys are coming out," Pierce said, and although he was clearly trying to be strong, she saw the strained look on his face, saw the way he held his side, and saw the line of blood making a slow path down his temple.

"Pierce, you're bleeding," she said.

"Man, sit down and take it easy," Malice said and helped the prospect down to the ground.

"This was no accident, Malice," Pierce said with a hard tone. "That explosion was done by those fucking fanatics." Pierce exhaled roughly and closed his eyes. "My fucking head is killing me."

"Man, just relax. The ambulance will be here, and you can get you checked out, brother."

Pierce nodded. The ambulance and a few cop cars pulled up about fifteen minutes later, and then the rest of The Brothers of Menace were pulling in also. The police kept everyone back and away from the fire as it was trying to be put out, and then for the next twenty minutes the cops were asking them questions.

Adrianna was checked over by the paramedics, as was Pierce, and when he refused to go to the hospital all of the bikers gathered together.

"The women are at the clubhouse with Tuck and Ruin, so they are all okay, but fuck," Lucien said and looked at the building. The flames were slowly being extinguished, and even from the distance she could still feel the heat as if she was right in the thick of it.

"It was that fucking cult," Pierce said. "It has to be." He had a bandage on his head. "They dropped off those damn papers at the clubhouse, and then had the balls to come here a couple of weeks ago, and now this shit. This isn't a coincidence."

"Pierce is right," Malice said and pulled her close. He kissed her on the top of the head again. "No way this shit just happened, but why did they wait two damn weeks?"

"I don't think people that are fucking insane like that have any reasoning for why they do the shit they do," Lucien said on a growl, and she could tell he was barely hanging on to his control as it was. All of the guys seemed like they were ready to murder someone.

"It doesn't fucking matter though, because no one messes with the club and gets away with it." Lucien turned and stared at each of the guys.

"And we all know that once someone fucks with us or anyone that we consider under our protection, we won't let them walk away alive." Malice was the one to speak now.

All the guys murmured in agreement.

A shiver worked through her body at the lethalness that came from all of the bikers. "I did find a church paper on the porch right before Malice showed up." She looked up at Malice. "I think it was from The Church of the Good and Right, or Only, or Holy. I don't know. It was something like that."

There was a chorus of curses from the bikers.

"This is fucked up, and we need to retaliate," Rock said on a growl.

Lucien held up his hand. "I agree, but we need to think this through. I don't want the cops getting involved with this, because we don't need any more heat," Lucien said and glanced at the building again. "But I want to make sure it was the cult, even if I'd bet my fucking life on it." Lucien looked back at them, and the look on his face was deadly calm. "We are going to demolish that fucking cult and the one they call a leader."

They all murmured their agreement, and then Lucien, Ruin, and Rock headed back to their bikes. Malice tuned her around, cupped her face with his hands, and stared into her eyes.

"God, baby, for a moment there as I saw you lying there," he shook his head. "I thought I lost you." This pinched expression covered his face, and she lifted her hand and smoothed her fingers between his eyes.

"I'm glad everyone came out of it okay."

He leaned down and kissed her hard, and she could feel the possession in it. "I love you. *Christ*, I love you, baby." He tightened his hands on her face, and rested his forehead on hers.

"I love you, too, Malice."

He pulled back and looked into her face. "God, I would fucking do anything in my power to make sure you're protected, and to make you happy, baby."

She smiled and rested her head on his chest again.

"And I am going to fucking kill the ones that even dared to put you in danger."

She wrapped her arms around him, still resting her head on his chest, and closed her eyes.

"If something happened to you…" He held her tightly, and she heard the pain in his voice.

"Let's not think or talk about it."

"Okay, baby." He pulled back and kissed her again. "But this shit with that fucking cult isn't over with. They followed us up here, probably knowing we had the girls from Fairview with us, and wanted to make their deranged ideals known." He shook his head and clenched his jaw. "And when you mess with the fucking Brothers of Menace, you better be prepared to fall hard." He kissed her yet again, as if cementing his words as a decree.

Adrianna didn't doubt him for one minute, but she knew that as long as she had Malice with her, the women that had become her family, and The Brothers of Menace, she could handle anything. She had already been to hell and back, had even survived this far, and she wasn't about to be a victim again. No, she was a survivor, and that was how she wanted it to stay.

The End

**www.jenikasnow.com**

JENIKA SNOW

**EVERNIGHT PUBLISHING ®**

www.evernightpublishing.com

www.ingramcontent.com/pod-product-compliance
Lightning Source LLC
Chambersburg PA
CBHW022111170626
46808CB00002B/696